Ψ The Devil's Inbox

The Devil's Inbox

Ψ

by Barbara Laymon

Augsburg Books
MINNEAPOLIS

THE DEVIL'S INBOX

Large-quantity purchases or custom editions of this book are available at a discount from the publisher. For more information, contact the sales department at Augsburg Fortress, Publishers, 1-800-328-4648, or write to: Sales Director, Augsburg Fortress, Publishers, P.O. Box 1209, Minneapolis, MN 55440-1209.

ISBN 0-8066-4945-3

Cover design by Brad Norr Design
Book design by Michelle L. N. Cook

The paper used in this publication meets the minimum requirements of American National Standard for Information Sciences—Permanence of Paper for Printed Library Materials, ANSI Z329.48-1984. ∞ ™

Manufactured in the U.S.A.

07   06   05   04   03   1   2   3   4   5   6   7   8   9   10

Table of Contents

For Vicki and Chris

Acknowledgments

Litany of a first-time author:

For my editors and all who have participated in taking me from crayons to a book, especially Renni Browne, Michael Wilt, David Hitchcock, and the staff at Augsburg.

For spiritual mentors, especially Richard Smith, Becky Wright, George Bunn, George Glazier, Sylvia Williams, Park Bodie, L.D. Johnson, and Betty Alverson.

For the teachers who began my instruction in the craft of writing, and the immeasurable patience their work requires, especially Duncan McArthur and Robert ("Skeet") Willingham.

For all who encouraged me to keep writing, especially Tom Rybolt, Ann Rybolt, George Connor, Chris Bryan, Amanda Wynn, Mary Lib Randall, Rebecca Williams, Ann Swint, Joy Jones, Mary Hatzikazakis, and Darla Freehardt.

For those who have allowed me to be with them in difficult times, especially my sister, Vicki Randall; my father, Ed Pasco; and my friend, Chris Presley. They fought the good fight, finished the race, and kept the faith in ways that inspired me to live and write more fully.

For friends who have brought perspective and laughter into my life. Their contributions are sprinkled all over these pages.

For family who were always there for me, especially my mother, Marilyn Pasco, and my brother, Doug Pasco.

For my husband, Paul, and our children, Matt, Katie, and Anna, and their countless kindnesses while I worked on this project.

I give you thanks, O God.

How often would I have gathered your children together
as a hen gathers her brood under her wings,
and you would not.

(Matthew 23:37)

Preface

One sleepy morning, sipping my first cup of coffee as I signed on to check my e-mail, a snarly but seductive voice said, "Welcome! You've got Hell." Suddenly wide awake, coffee sloshing everywhere, I found myself reading correspondence from an elderly advisor named Anesthesia to a junior tempter on her first assignment. When the screen began blurring I somehow thought to hit the print command. The next thing I knew my computer was crashing and burning—and I was holding on to the letters that follow here.

Letters from an exceptionally clever devil once fell into the hands of C. S. Lewis, who chronicled them in *The Screwtape Letters*. I first read *Screwtape* when I was seventeen, and over the years it has become a good friend—entertaining, understanding, and enlightening. Whether the reader has also enjoyed *Screwtape* or is new to the genre of these devilish writings, Anesthesia's letters may shed some light on the diabolical difficulties of leading a spiritual life today.

After reading Anesthesia's letters a few times, I began to notice the most disconcerting and dismaying similarities between her and me on a bad day. Exactly how her letters might speak to theological views about the nature of evil, Jungian concepts of the shadow side, dualism, or other constructs for all that has gone wrong in the world, I can't say. I can't even understand how, after years—decades—of prayer, study, fellowship, and worship, I find myself identifying with a devil. What is this power over me, or is it within me, or is it both? More generally, what makes people go wrong? It's an ancient question, recently featured on the cover of *Newsweek* (May 21, 2001), set to a reddish background, a haunted face, and the word EVIL writ large. And the briefest consideration of recent history makes it abundantly clear that we are no closer than the ancients to answering it.

What's also clear is that I'm part of the problem. With the Apostle Paul I despair to find that when I try to do good, evil lies close at hand. It draws me inexorably and attracts me irresistibly—at first. With time, evil does seem to lose its luster. And like Peter when the cock crowed, ultimately I recognize that I have lost my way. Although evil can entice me, eventually it sickens and repels me.

Eventually. Like a fly in a spider's web, by the time I figure out what's happened to me, I'm in real trouble. Anesthesia's h-mails have helped me to spot the webs—sometimes not getting quite so tangled up in them before I see my folly, occasionally avoiding them altogether. With God's help, I hasten to add, with God and with a sense of humor. Somehow the power of evil intensifies when I take it too seriously. And it quickly overwhelms me when I forget God. Oddly enough, God is sprinkled all through Anesthesia's letters,* suggesting that even the forces of Hell must reflect on the Almighty if they are to gain any perspective on life.

Perspective—the psalmist's prayer to set me on the rock that is higher than I—seems to me to be the beginning of understanding. With perspective comes detachment and eventually abandonment to divine providence, a place where evil can find no foothold. But how do we get there? The saints say it's easy and maybe it would be, if only we could let go of all that keeps us from God. But at least for me, that's more than a pretty big *if*—it's a huge, a seemingly impossible, a not-in-this-life *if*. And so I hold fast to the idea that in the end, nothing will come between us and the love of God, and look for clues on finding that abundant life now. My old companion Anesthesia has given some hints, but I must warn you about her. She tends to overestimate her own importance, power, and understanding of the world. Weigh her words carefully, for sometimes she deceives even herself.

*The metaphor of Mother Hen (the MH) is taken from Jesus' words in Matthew 23:37.

ψ Part One

Subj: Hello and welcome to my fine family of advisees
From: Anasty1
To: gnawingirl (Termite N. Fester)

My dear Termite—What a pleasure to have you on board, and so highly recommended from the Academy. And what a choice assignment you've been given in that young middle-class human. My dear, she'll be too *busy* to notice herself headed straight to us, ripe for our eternal consumption. All you'll have to do is guide her on her journey. And I'll be here to advise you every step of the way.

    Ψ Anesthesia

Subj: Don't get giddy
From: Anasty1
To: gnawingirl

Hold on, now. Your human should be a simple matter, that much is certain. But you will still have to contend with Her—our sworn enemy—clucking around her witless human chicks. The Mother Hen* is always ready to gather them under Her wings—always willing to comfort, renew, and strengthen them. It's simply *tacky*, the way She loves Her creation, especially that gaudy rainbow-colored planet and its chaotically confused population of bipeds with souls.

    Ψ Anesthesia

Subj: The good news
From: Anasty1
To: gnawingirl

Unlike birds in a barnyard, the humans don't have enough *sense* to follow their own MH around. As for your intended victim's occasional church attendance, I doubt that it has anything to do with following the

* See Matthew 23:37.

Mother Hen. Probably just another young human worshipping her own opinions, combining narcissism with a drop of idealism.

But just to make sure that church doesn't ever become a problem for us, try my proven technique: Compartmentalizing. She has college and work and friends and church. . . . *Make sure these categories are kept separate in her mind.* At work no one talks about church, so at church no one talks about work, etc., etc. If she lived in a village where everyone gathered around the campfire to celebrate festivals, or even in a time and place where life for the entire community revolved around a single religious calendar, it would be harder for her to sort out her life into categories. But in her world, where one place has nothing to do with another, the separation of church and life gives us a real edge. She can go all week without ever once thinking of the place!

Once her churchgoing is separate from whatever she does all week, it's an easy leap to placing the Mother Hen Herself in a special, holy category: separate from the rest of the week. Let your victim think of Her as a very busy super-human, with lots of important matters on Her mind. Suggest that she should reserve her prayers for "really serious" problems, that the MH "shouldn't be bothered" with her little worries.

Ψ Anesthesia

Subj: A model of etiquette
From: Anasty1
To: gnawingirl

Relax. The MH won't bother your victim. Oh no, not Her—She never henpecks, you know. It's part of Her silly strategy that She won't even begin to let Her presence be known unless She's invited to do so. Fortunately we feel no similar compunction to play by the rules.

Ψ Anesthesia

Subj: Surely you jest
From: Anasty1
To: gnawingirl

Some nerdy professor at the Academy who's never worked a day in the real world questioned the efficacy of my brilliant compartmentalizing strategy? And *you* wonder whether the presence of the MH at all times and in all places isn't so clear that your victim can't help noticing? Both of you need a little reality orientation, if you ask me. Each and every human is far too wrapped up in herself to see the obvious.

   Ψ Anesthesia

Subj: You don't have to explain anything
From: Anasty1
To: gnawingirl

Leave logic to the MH, who is unfailingly logical, truthful, etc. with the humans. What a mistake! Does She really think the humans want to know the *truth* about life? That they want to hear, for instance, that they aren't in control? Or that life involves suffering? Please! And if you think your victim might figure out an idea like infinity—that the MH can be everywhere, always—my, my, you do have a lot to learn, don't you. Although there have been some unfortunate incidents within the scientific community, most humans go along foolishly assuming that the entire universe operates according to the apparent rules of their little planet. Keep her in ignorance, Termite, *that's* your job.

   Ψ Anesthesia

Subj: Opportunity abounds!
From: Anasty1
To: gnawingirl

Termite—Now we're getting somewhere: not just a boyfriend, but a boyfriend she's crazy about. Wonderful! I know, I know—only too well—what you are thinking. To us pure spirits, sexuality looks like a dull theater of operations. But through it we can corrupt her whole life.

Your work has been made all the easier by your victim's culture. Thanks to the many years between adolescence and the time considered acceptable for marriage, young humans are walking containers of lust—it's that simple. Now, as you put it so well, she wants to think of nothing else but her boyfriend and what they do together. It's your job to make sure she relives again and again every moment of it. And make sure she has plenty to think about. Get with her boyfriend's tempter—get with her boyfriend's roommate's tempter, for that matter, have the roommate lured away from the room with keg stands and casinos. Once they're alone, whisper to her that it's just cuddle time and take it from there.

Ψ Anesthesia

Subj: Let them wallow in it
From: Anasty1
To: gnawingirl

I *know* it's incredibly tedious, but the great—and in my opinion, unrecognized—value of sex outside of marriage remains. It's so *distracting*. She can think endlessly about what they did last night, and was it too frustrating for him, or what they may do next weekend, and whether or not it's right or wrong, and does he really love her . . . ad nauseum. *What a waste of her time!* It is the exact opposite of the sort of sexual life the MH blesses, which would have her walking around glowing, with more energy for every task and more love to spread around as a consequence of *being* loved.

No, what you're after is a sex life that is a dissipating, enervating, weakening of her young vitality. We have turned around many a young, promising life in just this fashion.

Ψ Anesthesia

Subj: Wake up and smell the coffee
From: Anasty1
To: gnawingirl

Termite—Have you been paying attention here? You don't have to be logical. It's amazing, but humans can look at geese and say, "how lovely, they mate for life," and yet we can easily convince them to sleep with anything that attracts them. Besides, how hard can it be to tempt a human to do what she already wants to do?

Now, sexual sins are small potatoes; the MH will forgive them in Her usual indiscriminate style. The point is to use sin to keep your victim from communicating with Her at all. Who wants to confess a sin she's unwilling to stop? Or one she's unwilling to stop considering!? If it occurs to her that somehow what she's doing has become a barrier between her and the MH, drop the word "freedom" into her consciousness. Of course she must be free! She hears it in her religion; she hears it in her culture—fortunately for us, she has no idea of what it *means*.

Ψ Anesthesia

Subj: Freedom and other theoretical possibilities
From: Anasty1
To: gnawingirl

The free human, while not extinct, is a very rare bird indeed. (And very offensive, too.) If you ever spot one, you'll know it, for she'll stand out like a flat-billed platypus crossing Main Street. But she doesn't have to walk—she soars on Her repulsive wings of trust and surrender.

Ψ Anesthesia

Subj: No way
From: Anasty1
To: gnawingirl

For a human to fly, she must start practicing some short leaps of faith—she must at least *begin* trying to do things the MH's way and trusting Her with the rest. Not to worry, most humans—yours included, I'm sure—quite naturally prefer to look out for their own interests according to their own methods; thus not only providing but also maintaining and ever reinforcing their own prisons. Train yours to follow the devices and desires of her own heart, under the guise of freedom, and she'll never realize that her own passions enslave her.

Slaves! Ours or the MH's, there's really no in between. Yes, yes, She tells them that if they'll follow Her and Her ways, they'll be free to be themselves. Really, Termite, it's no wonder the humans don't practice what they preach. Who could possibly relate to the perversely paradoxical style of the MH?

Ψ Anesthesia

Subj: Delightful to watch
From: Anasty1
To: gnawingirl

Are you, perhaps, just the tiniest bit envious of her boyfriend's tempter? (Don't be, my dear. He is, after all, a senior devil, and we are presumed to know a little something!) On balance, I'd say he's doing an excellent job. Just listen to the boyfriend's incessant whining about his needs—why, I'd guess he has just about convinced your victim that she is being unkind to deny him her body! I doubt it will take much to encourage her to give way—the young, hot-blooded little animal. I look forward to the day when we have her here, where we can alternate between heating up her lustful desires, sucking the life force from them, and then throwing her in the frigid lake.

Ψ Anesthesia

Subj: Get a grip
From: Anasty1
To: gnawingirl

Oh please, Termite. Tempting feckless fornicators to forget or forego birth control is not exactly an original idea, after all. And the consequences are far more complicated than you realize. Pregnancy is not guaranteed, you know. And should it happen, abortion is not her only choice. What if she gives the little brat away to some lonely humans who would treasure and nurture the child—do you want *that* on your record? I know I don't want it on mine.

Ψ Anesthesia

Subj: Abort this plan
From: Anasty1
To: gnawingirl

I'm guessing that you've been influenced by stories like the one in the latest *Hellish Times* about the admirably self-centered college sophomore who said, "I had to have an abortion, the baby was due the week of my finals." Have you heard about the special exam being prepared for her anticipated arrival here below? Let's just say these are multiple-choice exercises she won't soon forget. . . .

But back to earth: many humans who have abortions will, sooner or later, feel remorse—real, true, undeniable remorse. Who needs *that*? The next thing you know, the MH is forgiving them—and then they're even closer to Her than ever before. Besides, it absolutely sickens me to watch an abortion. The tiny human with that spark of eternity, heading straight for the MH—and we don't even have a sporting chance to make the soul our own.

Ψ Anesthesia

Subj: Take it from me. . .
From: Anasty1
To: gnawingirl

. . . and keep it between us, please—abortions are simply more trouble than they're worth. I know they're all the rage at the lowest level of policy making, but that's what you have an advisor *for*, Termite. Applied tempting differs from theoretical policy. I can't be responsible if you attempt to implement your academic ideas on earth.

    Ψ Anesthesia

Subj: One thing you could do with abortion
From: Anasty1
To: gnawingirl

What if you let her take a stand on the issue? Yes, that's it. Encourage her to become ardently right-to-life or radically pro-choice. Or some other issue, it doesn't much matter. Laws for or against homosexuals, or capital punishment. Or some environmental issue—the right to grow dandelions in the suburbs, I don't care, just as long as she burns with the righteous zeal of the 100 percent correct. Lead her to reading materials and acquaintances who support her preconceived biases—no, bombard her until she's incapable of hearing, much less understanding, the other side.

    Ψ Anesthesia

Subj: It's not rocket science
From: Anasty1
To: gnawingirl

Can you really not see the benefits? Once she quits listening to any voice but her own and others who agree with her, you can chain her with her own intensity. What fun to contemplate her eternal future here, placed in the most confining of prisons with precisely those humans she could least abide on earth. Their passionate hatred for one another fuels the flames of Hell, in an energy-efficient economy without parallel in the universe.

Ψ Anesthesia

Subj: Like everything else in heaven and on earth
From: Anasty1
To: gnawingirl

All the humans' moral and ethical issues become part of the MH's tiresome approach of giving them infinite opportunity to understand and love each other. The MH Herself has been rumored to seat former opponents together at the banquet table of heaven, in Her perpetual quest for perfect communion. Make sure you do the opposite. Keep your charge in places where everybody agrees with her, fooling her into thinking that she's in a real community. True community comes about only when the humans can disagree—passionately, sometimes—yet still care for one another. We have a much simpler task: get them to disagree on some issue and develop hatred and division around it.

Ψ Anesthesia

Subj: Try this for a little added spark
From: Anasty1
To: gnawingirl

You might even encourage her to search through the scriptures for passages that support her own position. There's always the danger that she might absorb something life-giving, but the risk is minuscule when a close-minded human reads in order to prove (to herself and others) that she's correct. Listening openly is a prerequisite for understanding anything. And the MH does have followers (often on both sides of an issue) who have learned to set aside their own views, trying to comprehend Her and each other as well. Suggest to your victim that such a humble posture is meek, weak, "not taking a stand," etc.

Ψ Anesthesia

Subj: Think positive
From: Anasty1
To: gnawingirl

Termite—enough with the yes, buts—it's time you learned about tempting in the real world. The general theoretical rule on avoiding scripture has some exceptions in practice, and finding proof texts to support an issue is a clear exception. *It is but one short step to scripture-as-weapon!*

Ψ Anesthesia

Subj: Your place in a wonderful tradition
From: Anasty1
To: gnawingirl

I trust you memorized all those time lines at the Academy. If so, you're aware of the Schism Department's long history of using intolerance to advantage in organized religion, with holy wars, the Inquisition, and various pogroms all to their credit. Might it be possible to start a small holy war within your victim's congregation? I know she only attends occasionally, but sometimes that's the best type to really stir things up. To determine the most likely topic for divisiveness in her denomination, check with Enmity, a colleague of mine over in Schism's Section for Furthering Discord. It wouldn't hurt your career, Termite, for your first victim to become a strident supporter of a hot-button issue: hot enough to tear her congregation in two.

Ψ Anesthesia

Subj: Sorry, Charlie
From: Anasty1
To: gnawingirl

World hunger, according to the Standards on Strategies in 21st Century Temptation, is technically classified as a Cause—unlike the controversial issue I had in mind, it won't work to cause divisiveness in her church. After all, what human would claim to be *for* world hunger?

Still, it may do. . . . Tell me more. Does a picture of a hungry child, belly swollen, bring tears to her eyes? Does she turn off the evening news at the first shot of drought and famine? These are your moments, Termite, to confuse her. A loving deity couldn't possibly allow such horrors. Convince her that her faith just doesn't make sense.

Ψ Anesthesia

Subj: What she can't see can't hurt us
From: Anasty1
To: gnawingirl

Remember her narrow vantage point. She's stuck in time, Termite; and one grim, sad scene can overwhelm her. She's never seen the whole picture: mouth-watering tragedy all too briefly displayed on earth, followed by a disgusting, revolting, never-ending show of joy in heaven. It's all upside down: the worse off they were on earth, the more quickly they are ready to receive what heaven has to offer. But your victim has no concept of "the last shall be first," and no way, under her own power, of having faith in the MH's way of doing things.

Probably she does have some vague idea that suffering and death came into the world through the event known as "the Fall." But she fails to see what the MH was really up to. Your human is clueless, and if you know your business, you'll keep her that way.

Ψ Anesthesia

Subj: It was a setup
From: Anasty1
To: gnawingirl

No mother bakes a batch of chocolate chip cookies, puts them right in the middle of the kitchen table, points to the cookies, tells her children, "Don't eat these," and then disappears from their sight—unless she wants the cookies to disappear before dinner. The MH *wanted* the humans to eat the fruit, to gain the knowledge of good and evil.

Ψ Anesthesia

Subj: She who laughs last . . .
From: Anasty1
To: gnawingirl

What happened in the garden will ultimately serve our purposes, not Hers. Her misguided effort to allow the miserable human creatures the freedom to decide whether or not to sin—whether to live with or without Her—has led to all our glorious opportunities for evil. The suffering, pain, misery, and anguish of life on earth *grieve* the MH—more, I'm pleased to say, than your victim could possibly imagine.

Ψ Anesthesia

Subj: Unusual is an understatement
From: Anasty1
To: gnawingirl

"Weird" doesn't cover it, Termite. The very idea that She would allow part of herself to take bodily form: *bizarre*. That Her Son would participate in the suffering and death of the world: *grotesque*. And it's reliably reported that Her Son continues to suffer with every moment of suffering on Earth. This way of doing business is *crazy*, if you ask me; but then again, She's always been so *incomprehensible,* Termite. Our More

Exalted Mother below removed herself from the presence of the MH over an argument on just this topic.

Ψ Anesthesia

Subj: It's not that simple
From: Anasty1
To: gnawingirl

She's still plotting against us. Forget whatever doctrine is currently being espoused—I've seen a lot of them come and go. All we really know is that through the event known as the Cross, She somehow managed to create good from evil and to start making all things better than they would have been if the world had never gone wrong.

Her ridiculous claim? *That all things—including us, mind you—all things in the created universe have been, are being, and will be redeemed.* Absurd! Well, it *is* true that anyone who wants redeeming has only to ask, that anyone who prays for a situation to be redeemed can be certain that the prayer will be answered, etc., etc. ad nauseum. But since we will never, *never, never* ask for such a thing, the MH's plan is sure to fail. What a *pathetic* existence, open to whatever happens, depending on the MH to make it all better. Make sure your victim recoils at the very thought of such a childish approach to life.

Ψ Anesthesia

Subj: Your future
From: Anasty1
To: gnawingirl

Of course I have the highest regard for the Doctrinal Command and the most recent revisions concerning the Fall. As for your questions about the apparent inconsistencies in my comments, be assured that I am *not* offended. I can see that the Tempter's Academy has again sent me one of their brightest graduates—most gratifying to find you up on the latest canons on Unredemption. Let me hasten to add that I'm in complete agreement and cooperation with everything promulgated at the last Convention. My record is spotless—any confusion on my theoretical positions was inadvertent.

You could request an advisor, of course, with more of a flare for the theoretical, although that might not be in your best interests in the long run. My expertise in applied tempting has yielded the highest success rate among new tempters anywhere, anytime. It's up to you; certainly, many more tempters want your slot. But if you want an eternity to enjoy your victim, better stick with me for now.

Ψ Anesthesia

Subj: Family Secrets
From: Anasty1
To: gnawingirl

Let's just forget all that confusion of our last correspondence. I *do* consider you a close relation: a niece, perhaps. While you're with me, I treat you like family—and you become my family, part of a long tradition of excellence in tempting. I share with you my family recipes, shall we say, on preparing a delicious human dish for our table. Of course these are our secret recipes, designed to be used only with tempters who've had the careful training, which only I can give. I'm sure I needn't tell you that my advice is for you and you alone.

Ψ Anesthesia

Subj: I agree completely
From: Anasty1
To: gnawingirl

I think perhaps we've been saying the same thing. *Of course.* It simply can't be that the MH wants to associate with the humans as free creatures. Why want free creatures when She had contented slaves? The very idea that She loves them is ludicrous. It's only a matter of time before research (or espionage) yields to us what She is really doing with them. But in the meantime we must face the appalling reality that, for whatever reason, the MH is trying to draw all things to Herself.

Ψ Anesthesia

Subj: Enough of chit-chat
From: Anasty1
To: gnawingirl

I can only talk for so long before I'm itching to get back to work. You'll find your victim extraordinarily ignorant about redemption. If she thinks about it at all, she thinks it means that she (personally) has been saved from her sins. Be that as it may (or may not) the MH intends something much broader than the personal salvation of a relatively few fortunate souls. Why, only just today I saw a sign in front of a church advertising a sermon titled "Making Easter Work for You." Do you see how wrong the humans have it? As if Easter were made to work for a few who have somehow it figured out!

Through Easter, the MH means to redeem it all, every last drop of Her creation, every single tear that has fallen throughout the universe. The baptized ones are marked by the MH as a special work force in this incredible, absurd project. Be assured, Termite, that She will fail. For your part, keep your victim in blissful ignorance about redemption.

Instead, fuel her anger at the injustices of the world. (You certainly don't lack for material!) Tell her that surely the MH could have created a different world, a world where things could not go so wrong. *Just don't let her consider the logical extension of a "better" world: a Creator arranging every moment of Her creatures' existence.* Encourage her to reject the MH's gift of free will, a gift for which her Son paid a huge price in that futile effort to redeem. If she concludes that suffering shows life is not to be trusted, she'll be easily convinced that the Author of life is not to be trusted.

Ψ Anesthesia

Subj: Stop her
From: Anasty1
To: gnawingirl

Anger can be useful to us, yes—*if and only if* you make sure she never expresses her outrage directly to the MH. The MH doesn't mind wrestling with the humans. On the contrary, she seems to enjoy conflict as a way to make Herself known to them. No, you want your victim to become stubborn, withdrawn, and isolated from the MH. Convince her that the MH obviously doesn't care about the poor, the hungry; that there's no sense in talking to Her about it.

Ψ Anesthesia

Subj: Don't stop now
From: Anasty1
To: gnawingirl

Nice going. So now you finish her off. Spark a faith crisis: The world is clearly rife with hatred and injustice. The idea of a just and loving deity is clearly a myth (implying, of course, falsehood—not myth as deeper truth). Convince her that the problem's too big, nothing she can do will alleviate it, so she might as well enjoy life. Idealism and concern for the poor *can* be replaced with materialism and cynicism.

Ψ Anesthesia

Subj: Other options
From: Anasty1
To: gnawingirl

Look, it was worth a try. If she (like many young humans) won't budge from her idealism, just build on it. Have you heard of the Crusader option? Once church becomes just another club where she can organize others to support her latest fundraising cause, you're halfway to getting her to substitute the cause for her religion. She'll continue to think she's somehow connected to the MH, while you continue to lead her further and further from Her.

One caveat: If a human is devoted to something the MH holds dear, She may (unfairly, I might add) count it as devotion to Her. Just one idea you must keep from your victim's mind—that she is to do what she can and then trust the MH with the rest. If this should occur to her, suggest that it would be yielding to *temptation* to think such a thing, that surely the MH expects more. They are so vain, Termite: so easily led to think that the weight of the world is on their shoulders.

    Ψ Anesthesia

Subj: Careful, now
From: Anasty1
To: gnawingirl

If she gets to know the people she's fighting for, she's exposed to powerless humans—the world's worst for the tendency to accept, even embrace, their own vulnerability. The MH Herself tends to prefer the poor, and will always be hanging around. No, you want to keep her safe in that middle-class world of hers. If she's going to be a Crusader, you must lead her to do it without her actually spending *any* time with the poor or the sick or the disabled or the imprisoned. They might rub off on her.

    Ψ Anesthesia

Subj: What's the problem?
From: Anasty1
To: gnawingirl

It should be easy to convince her that fundraising will do more good than ladling soup. Talk to her about the importance of efficiency, and the economy of heaven will never occur to her. And someday, the effectiveness of our crowd control methods will leave a rather lasting impression, I'm sure.

Ψ Anesthesia

Subj: As always, the boyfriend could help
From: Anasty1
To: gnawingirl

Why not talk with his tempter about a nasty little breakup? Something along the lines of, "You know, I'm concerned about the poor, but I want to have some fun, too. I've been a good sport, but enough is enough." A loss of faith in the MH combined with loss of a lover—now that's a picture fit for a demon.

Ψ Anesthesia

Ψ Part Two

Subj: Not exactly original, but a proven record of success
From: Anasty1
To: gnawingirl

While she's getting over her boyfriend, try connecting her with those people at her office who go out for a drink every night after work. She might not care much for the drinking part at first, just go along with it to be a part of the group. But if you could get her started, she might soon begin to look forward to the drink itself. Then increase the quantity, etc. It's worth a shot.

Ψ Anesthesia

Subj: They are different, you know.
From: Anasty1
To: gnawingirl

How *did* you get through Tempter's Academy without a working familiarity with the concept and practice of Human Differentiation? You can't tempt her to become an alcoholic in the same way you might work with a drunken sailor, for crying out loud. If she doesn't feel well after an evening of bar-hopping and has just about given up drinking except on special occasions, that's *your* doing, Termite. You went too fast.

But all is not lost on the addictive front. Many a soul has begun her journey here by first devoting herself to something simple, like television or cigarettes. Other obvious choices include drugs (illegal or prescription), gambling, work, even shopping. And what about the Internet? It's so enjoyable to watch an unsuspecting human get more and more tangled up in the web.

Ψ Anesthesia

Subj: You'll be glad you did
From: Anasty1
To: gnawingirl

Granted, developing an addiction is hard work—but consider the ever-lasting future with your victim. Think of her, here with us, completely under our control forever. Be ambitious, Termite. Don't forget what you are after: the life force of a human, with all that incredible, unending energy at the core. You can enjoy her forever, feasting when you wish, maybe snacking a little at other times. I always enjoy the dinner conversation as I indulge myself on our victims, especially when I'm familiar with the details of how they came to us. The absolute horror on their faces as we discuss their pathetic little lives! I am eager for her, Termite. My size and power require constant nourishment. Bring her to us, we must have her. But we indulge ourselves on her later. For now, there's work to be done.

ᴪ Anesthesia

Subj: Eating—it's everywhere you want to be
From: Anasty1
To: gnawingirl

I like it. The human body, more adapted to times of famine than times of plenty, doesn't know when to quit eating. Your victim has to have some food—she can't ever simply swear off of it. It's ubiquitous in her world, she can't get away from it. And she seems inclined that way already—a very good sign. You want to hook her while she's still young, and can live with any related physical problems that might keep her from going to extremes in later years. It's a good idea—likely to help place her on our menu, someday.

A pleasure to watch your developing abilities, Termite.

ᴪ Anesthesia

Subj: Now we're cooking
From: Anasty1
To: gnawingirl

Here's the beauty of the whole addictive scenario. It was the MH Herself who made the humans with a longing for Her. The humans recognize a longing, an emptiness—but they are too witless to know what *for*. All their feelings, if properly attended to, would lead them back to the MH. But when your victim gets tired, let's say, or lonely, or afraid, or angry or any of the 1,001 sensations the MH created her to be capable of—then you put it in her mind that a little snack would be just the thing. When she's feeling happy or satisfied or simply pleased with herself, she might be led to celebrate with a second dessert. Help her to interpret every feeling as signaling a need to eat instead of pointing to a need for the MH, and voila: she comes to an absolute dependence on food and complete ignorance of what the MH has to offer. We can beat Her at her own game, Termite. We are doing so every day.

Ψ Anesthesia

Subj: Get used to it
From: Anasty1
To: gnawingirl

So what else is new? The MH is always doing *something* that gets their attention. Admittedly, it can interfere with our plans. I've seen a hardened cynic crumble at the sight of one beautiful sunset. I've seen a victim in utter despair uplifted by a silly chirping bird. The slightest hint of the disgusting, blinding radiance of the MH, and years of our hard work can go down the drain—if *you* let her notice it.

Ψ Anesthesia

Subj: You can stop with the hysterics
From: Anasty1
To: gnawingirl

Of course it's possible to keep her from noticing the world around her. Just get her wondering what's for lunch.

Besides, you don't have to keep her from noticing *all* that is beautiful. Is she a visual person, or the musical type, or the kind who becomes aware of beauty through experience? Don't bother me with the theory that the MH made all the humans able to perceive Her in all ways. Few of them ever come near the point of using all their senses. If nothing boosts her spirits more than good music, make sure her CD player is broken. If a long soak in a hot tub pleases her to no end, make sure her hot water heater is small. You get the idea. Avoid what is lovely for *her*.

   Ψ Anesthesia

Subj: Anything but this, anytime but now
From: Anasty1
To: gnawingirl

Come now, Termite, even the humans are on to this trick. Changing the subject is the bulwark of Western civilization. If the utter loveliness of the MH captures her attention, redirect it to how rude that person was to her at the bank this morning, or what she will say to her boyfriend tonight. Turn a beautiful drive into the countryside into an opportunity to reflect on what might have been, or to fret over what might be. Keep her reliving and resenting the past, or worrying over the future—anything but noticing the Present.

The humans who begin focusing on the Present, on what is happening to them in the Now, are the ones we have the most trouble with. They notice not only the MH's profligate outpouring of Herself in the world around them but also Her voice within them. These humans, even when put in the most dreary of circumstances, refuse to be confined. They have practiced noticing the MH and—well, like one of our magicians—they can almost make Her appear. But it isn't magic, it's the MH within, making Herself known in and through them. I recall one of Her prizes, why, she could (and did) make a prison cell seem warm and inviting. But your victim is a different story. The time will come when we will have her here, where she will never see another sunset, nor smell a rose, nor hold a baby . . . let's just see the MH try to reach her *then*.

Ψ Anesthesia

Subj: A well-kept (?) secret
From: Anasty1
To: gnawingirl

Don't know how you heard, but yes. Even in Hell we have the occasional (however infrequent) case of a human who remembers something of beauty. A very few have actually escaped us by recollecting past events where the MH's presence was clear. Humans anywhere who begin to contemplate how the MH was present to them one day can begin to realize how She was there another day, and another. . . . Eventually it becomes a habit they bring to the Present. For our purposes, any reflection on the Past must focus on what went wrong. When a human is well trained to look for our work, the MH will never be noticed at all.

Ψ Anesthesia

Subj: Just shift gears
From: Anasty1
To: gnawingirl

No, it wasn't bad advice. You simply must learn to adapt, Termite. Some humans aren't particularly interested in the past. No matter. Try the future. The MH isn't there either, you know. You might lead your victim to speculate on the perfect job, the perfect mate, anything. You might lead her to find no satisfaction in the present, substituting years of idle dreaming about what might be. Years, decades—a lifetime, even—can be spent without her ever noticing that the MH is right here, right now.

By the way, this technique may work well to keep your human from whatever vocation the MH is preparing her for. The MH may be showing her the next step, but if you keep her thinking ten years down the road, she'll miss the path right in front of her face.

Ψ Anesthesia

Subj: Like taking candy from a baby
From: Anasty 1
To: gnawingirl

Great work! A ten-year plan, with all her career goals mapped out in between?! Termite, that's *excellent* news. Successful humans are my favorites. They're so sure of their own power, so unlikely to thank the MH or to look to her for guidance. Quit worrying that she may actually contribute something to her world. You can count on the rest of us to make mincemeat out of anything she might accomplish. Let her work hard toward her goals; in fact, *encourage* her to produce.

Ψ Anesthesia

Subj: Let me count the lies
From: Anasty 1
To: gnawingirl

Productivity can put her on so many false roads, I hardly know where to begin. You might have her take pride in her efficiency (and then always find just a little something to criticize in everything she does). You might have her take pride in the sheer amount of work she can accomplish (and then always demand just a little more of herself). You might have her take pride in the work itself (and then see if you can't manage to have it taken from her). But all this is icing on the cake of their work ethic. The real game is to keep her too busy doing to find time for being—*until the day comes when having nothing to do frightens her more than anything.* Eventually she won't even recognize who she is if she doesn't have something to do.

Ψ Anesthesia

Subj: Choose her poison
From: Anasty1
To: gnawingirl

Now that you've made hard work such a part of her, it's time to branch out. In general, a human her age is still determining who she is, deciding things like, "I'm an outdoor person" or "I'm a couch potato." Encourage this. Don't let it enter her head that she could decide, "I'm no athlete, but I do like to get a walk in every day." Help her to avoid the middle way. What you want is for her to pick some qualities and exaggerate them, while pushing their opposites deep within her.

Ψ Anesthesia

Subj: There is one and only one exception
From: Anasty1
To: gnawingirl

Cheery or gloomy, who cares? *Any* quality that is exaggerated while its opposite is denied (with the single exception of unbounded love for the MH) is fodder for us. Some tendencies are easier to develop—all depends on what's in vogue in the culture—but *any* extreme will work.

The MH wants them to strike a balance. *She* would like for each person to be at peace within herself, listening to the many different voices inside and establishing an inner harmony. *We* want to keep them at war, not only with each other but also each human inside herself, unaware of the struggle and the undiscovered strengths within.

Ψ Anesthesia

Subj: Now you've gone too far
From: Anasty1
To: gnawingirl

Crowing over your victim's developing "little weight problem," as she calls it, is understandable. But goading her into a daily walk was ill-advised. You may have enjoyed watching her waddle up the street, on the verge of tears when she steps on the scale, but you were playing right into the hands of the MH. Don't you see that soon she might start to benefit from the walking and/or wake up to the fact that she needs to take better care of herself? The MH is always using some problem in the life of a human to warn her that she is heading the wrong way.

Besides, allowing these humans to exercise is against policy, and you know it. An exception is made in the case of those who might succumb to an exercise addiction, but your victim hardly fits those specs. These protocols were designed to *benefit* you inexperienced tempters—don't ignore them.

Ψ Anesthesia

Subj: Art appreciation
From: Anasty1
To: gnawingirl

You must begin to appreciate her culture, which has, among other highly desirable traits, the unique combination of the best medical care and the poorest health status ever known to humankind. It's a work of *art,* centuries in the making. Under the Long Lives, Lousy Lifestyles victim management approach, lulling the humans into a psychic stupor is a breeze. We keep them tired, moody, and irritable not through any fancy footwork but merely by making sure they eat the standard diet of the times, refrain from exercise, and fail to get enough sleep. You may think it a small thing, keeping your victim from walking or luring her into staying up late every night. But over the years, the accumulation in weariness may yield some exquisite results. The MH made her so that what she does with her body does affect her spirit. She's just an animal in clothes, Termite—and she *wants* you to help her forget it.

Ψ Anesthesia

Subj: How to break a good habit
From: Anasty1
To: gnawingirl

Very few of the humans can continue anything alone. Convince her that it's inconvenient to go walking with her friends, plant the notion that she might go by herself at another time. She'll drop it soon enough. Besides that, why should she have friends? Sounds like the MH is at work again.

Ψ Anesthesia

Subj: It wasn't easy, tempting back then
From: Anasty1
To: gnawingirl

Enough with your complaining, Termite. Back when exercise was part of human existence—when humans had to walk to the stream and haul in the water everyday—now that was tough going. You've got it made.

We didn't have anorexic young models, either. The admirable work of Leechlady and her crew in Fashion Design has elevated a body type rarely if ever found yet endlessly worshiped and desired. You *are* capitalizing on its constant exposure in movies and magazines, aren't you? And what about your victim's new boyfriend? Although the young stud may actually like her on the heavy side (our studies show many do), male humans are especially vulnerable to the visual coercion now available on television and many excellent Web sites as well. Have you discussed the case with his tempter? If her new flame begins teasing her about her weight, that could set in motion a delightful cycle of feeling depressed, eating more, and feeling more depressed.

Ψ Anesthesia

Subj: The tip of the iceberg
From: Anasty1
To: gnawingirl

I told you to have her look at the pictures in women's magazines, not scan the articles. You're the one who let her read "Ten Ways to Beat the Blues." And if you didn't think the MH would use something so trite, you have a lot to learn. The MH will stoop to anything. The problem goes way beyond your victim's feeling less depressed now. We can fix that. But her remembering the little tip about taking three deep breaths anytime she feels herself getting upset—now, that's unfortunate. Breathing techniques can make your victim temporarily immune to your suggestions. They can quiet her, relax her, even promote an inner stillness. Before long you'll have a good habit on your hands that's going to be hard to break.

Ψ Anesthesia

Subj: The tools at your disposal
From: Anasty1
To: gnawingirl

You've simply been taking it for granted that her exterior world is so noisy it's practically impossible for her to cultivate any sort of interior silence. You'd better squash that breathing foolishness, and squash it fast. Take advantage of the opportunity the Realm of Noise hands you, practically on a plate—why, your victim could live her whole life without ever hearing what she herself is thinking or feeling, much less noticing the MH.

Pagers, cell phones, answering machines, computers, not to mention CDs, DVDs, commuting with the car radio blasting. . . . What chance does she have for quiet?

Ψ Anesthesia

Subj: What do you think we did before radio?
From: Anasty1
To: gnawingirl

You seem to be losing a bit of control over her, Termite, and that could mean trouble ahead. But so what if she's turning the radio off on her drive to work? That doesn't in itself give her a chance to cultivate any interior quiet. Noisy thoughts, loud feelings—these are your true allies, the persistent internal rumblings of discontent. And she can't turn them off. In fact, the more she tries to disregard them the louder and more persistent they will become. Telling her that she can somehow enforce a sense of peace and quiet within is a long-range tool for distracting her from the MH's voice. To hear the still small voice of the MH at her own center, she must sift through all the rest, not ignore it.

Ψ Anesthesia

Subj: Another tool for distraction
From: Anasty1
To: gnawingirl

So she's "in love." What a surprise. And what a misnomer. It's got little to do with love and a lot to do with the mating instinct of all animals. The MH designed them this way (one assumes because She wants to ensure the continuation of this hapless, clueless species). But her preoccupation with her romance can become just another means of keeping her from hearing the MH.

And it will pass, her little happiness with her lover, it will pass. Our studies show that the humans tend to fall for just the sort of person who will cause them the most difficulty later on. Yours is no different, however much she seems to be enjoying herself now.

Ψ Anesthesia

Subj: If you want to ruin her fun
From: Anasty1
To: gnawingirl

And I can hardly blame you—why should she be allowed any pleasure? Try this angle. Part of the phenomena of being in love is the idolizing of the lover. Encourage this. Encourage her to see him as perfect, then later the reality of having married another imperfect human will be that much harder to bear. Not only that, but right now you can plant doubt in her mind about whether she "deserves" him. Find something she already feels uneasy about. Maybe the way she treated her mother or her sister as a child. Maybe a past relationship with another boyfriend—this would be an excellent time to plunge her into some remorse for one of those flings. Maybe something else, a test she cheated on, some drug use in younger days, betrayal of a friend—whatever you find, throw it in her face and suggest to her that she really isn't good enough for her lover. That should put a damper on things. She won't want to think about it, and that's half the fun. She won't want to listen to her conscience.

    Ψ Anesthesia

Subj: Get a spine
From: Anasty1
To: gnawingirl

March right back in there and take charge. Whoever told you that conscience is the MH's exclusive territory was dead wrong. And whoever told you the humans don't pay attention to the conscience any more has completely missed the point. When she discounts any suggestion from her conscience, we can use this to control her. The bothersome thought *will not go away*, as it would if she just stopped and dealt with it. Were she to face her conscience, she could benefit from it; that is, she could decide whether it was telling her something important or not. In this case, she could choose to talk with the MH about her past peccadilloes and then let go of them forever.

We, of course, want the opposite—a continual feeling of dis-ease with herself. And if you can make her upset with herself over something that doesn't bother the MH anyhow—or even better, over something She might approve of—then you have refined this method to the art form it can truly become.

 Ψ Anesthesia

Subj: Cheap grace
From: Anasty1
To: gnawingirl

Reassure her: "I'm okay." Or, "Everyone else was doing it." Or, "I shouldn't be hard on myself." The MH would be easier on her than she can imagine, but she'll never get far enough to find that out. Train her to expect forgiveness without confession. Although one of their theologians has guessed our strategy, we've managed to control the damage. Most of them think they can avoid guilt. In fact, they're so busy avoiding it that they avoid seeing the blindingly obvious: they must go through it before they can come out on the other side.

 Ψ Anesthesia

Subj: A complete triumph of our Linguistics Department
From: Anasty1
To: gnawingirl

While the word *sin* is unfashionable, the concept is at least as popular as ever. By all means keep her from talking in depth to anyone else—friend, counselor, or clergy—who might help her sort out when she is hearing the MH and when she is hearing us. Others, you see, could assist her in arriving at her own truth. Moreover, there's something about confessing to others that is extremely cleansing to the humans. We prefer keeping them feeling vaguely dirty.

 Ψ Anesthesia

Subj: Don't ask me how it works
From: Anasty1
To: gnawingirl

All I know is that breaking the humans from the habit of the confessional, whether in a formal or informal setting, gets my vote for the greatest achievement of the latest human millennium.

Ψ Anesthesia

Subj: How nice! A wedding to plan
From: Anasty1
To: gnawingirl

Don't be so obtuse. Surely you've heard of the Commission for Urging Romanticizing and Sentimentalizing on Earth (CURSE)? I can get more done at a wedding than I've ever accomplished at a funeral. The trouble with funerals is that the ones who are gathered usually consider, however briefly, their own mortality. At a wedding we do not have to be bothered with anything real. Well, I take that back, there is that business about vows to each other. But it's a piece of (wedding) cake to ensure that the vows are seen as a mere formality. Quaint, even sweet, but not *real* . . .

Ψ Anesthesia

Subj: Stay focused
From: Anasty1
To: gnawingirl

Your designs for the wedding are admirably diabolical, Termite. But what are you doing *right now*? You have a veritable feast of tension and stress set before you. All you have to do is see that the pressure of planning the perfect day never gives her the space to pray about how overwhelmed she's feeling in the present moment. If she must pray, keep any prayer focused on the future, where "bless my wedding day" soon leads her away from the MH and into wondering whether she remembered to talk to the caterer. That open-ended prayer "Thy will be done," the beginning point for the MH's work, should be the furthest thing from her mind.

Ψ Anesthesia

Subj: So many choices, so little time
From: Anasty1
To: gnawingirl

The only difficulty is choosing which "I-should-have" to make her feel bad about. How about this one. Let her beat herself up over forgetting to send an invitation to poor old Mrs. Smith, who probably couldn't care less, while being continually temperamental with her own mother, who couldn't be trying any harder. (It's an old trick, the least amount of concern over the most important relationships, and vice versa.) While the MH may be trying to speak to her about her mother, help your victim to ignore Her voice with a constant fusillade of petty thoughts. Little incidents like the oversight of poor old Mrs. Smith can help develop her sense of pride: "How *could* I forget her?"

Ψ Anesthesia

Subj: Amazing but true
From: Anasty1
To: gnawingirl

Calling poor old Mrs. Smith, apologizing, and inviting her at the last minute will never occur to her—unless you completely forget your work. Remember that she doesn't really care about poor old Mrs. Smith, she cares that she's made a mistake. Exploit the idiocy that she thinks she really could be perfect, that she's already close but not quite there. What she might call guilt is really embarrassment over her own behavior. She (like most humans) is in love with her ideal self and cannot bear to face reality. If she can't face reality, she certainly can't find the MH.

Ψ Anesthesia

Subj: Reality, humility, what's the difference?
From: Anasty1
To: gnawingirl

The reality is that a) the MH made them in Her own likeness, and b) She made them out of dirt. The latter ought to be enough to keep them firmly rooted in their own small place in the scheme of things, but believe me, they lack the humility to see life this way. The last thing they want to think about is that they will someday return to dust; and they're only too glad to have us lend support to the fiction that they have some control over it all. Puff yours up with pride, Termite, and bring her to us. We'll spend an eternity bursting her little bubble.

Ψ Anesthesia

Subj: Better nip this in the bud
From: Anasty1
To: gnawingirl

If you even *think* you've spotted a humble human (hh) anywhere near yours, you must find a way to put a stop to their relationship immediately. Here's what to look for. If her friend seems to have some perspective on the smallness of her world, forgetting to stay stuck in it, she might be an hh. If she doesn't take herself too seriously, she might be an hh. If she respects others—and their freedom—too much to insist on getting her own way, she might be an hh. If she looks at things in light of what the MH might be doing and offers her pathetic little life to become part of the MH's dreams, she might be an hh. Harrgh! Get your victim away from her!

It shouldn't be difficult to put some distance between them. Some little misunderstanding at the big event, perhaps, that you could blow all out of proportion. Then the excuse of her new marriage to keep her from making contact with her for a while. Finally she'll arrive at the place where she's really forgotten exactly what went wrong but is no longer comfortable thinking about her former friend. Before you know it, you've stopped the MH from working through another human. How sweet it is.

Ψ Anesthesia

Subj: The honeymoon's over
From: Anasty1
To: gnawingirl

Tempt your victim to think *it's her job to help her partner change*—after all, she already thinks she has a great deal of insight into her new spouse and knows what would be best for him. No human, of course, knows nearly as much as she thinks about her spouse, or any other human, for that matter. Many a long-term-miserable relationship begins with the proud and unquestioned assumption on one human's part that she understands the other.

Ψ Anesthesia

Subj: What did you expect?
From: Anasty1
To: gnawingirl

Of course each of them brings some genuine strengths to the marriage—all you have to do is keep your victim from valuing those her partner brings. Let her rationalize, resent, or at least minimize his good qualities. If she begins to respect him for them, that could lead to a habit of noticing good qualities and overlooking others. We want the opposite: *unreasonable expectations and continual disappointment* in the inadequacies of the other.

You will be amazed at how long—the rest of her life, possibly—your victim can continue to expect too much and then be disappointed in her mate.

ψ Anesthesia

Subj: Another match made in Hell
From: Anasty1
To: gnawingirl

Work with the dozens of small but promising issues of daily life between humans. They can irritate each other over everything from where the toothbrushes go to what to watch on television to when to take the trash out . . . the list is endless. You are coordinating with her husband's tempter, Licehead, aren't you? A little cooperation between the two of you could yield some big arguments between the two of them.

ψ Anesthesia

Subj: No triumph in itself
From: Anasty1
To: gnawingirl

Let me clarify. Other than some unkind words that may be hard to forget, arguing in itself does little to help our cause. In fact, it can lead to understanding among any two people who are making an effort to respect each other. *What you want is ongoing disagreements with no resolution.* Let them spend years—decades!—in which she turns the thermostat up and he turns it down, she puts the newspapers in the recycling bin and he takes them back out again, she wants to get there early and he dawdles until they're late. This is the sort of behavior that cheers us below—in which humans give up the chance for a lifetime of companionship, choosing instead a constant low-level power struggle.

ψ Anesthesia

Subj: If only
From: Anasty1
To: gnawingirl

Eventually your victim can be led to the "if only" point of view. If only he were _____, we could be happy. If only he did _____, I could be happy. It's a point of view with infinite possibilities. You can play the game with her every day, through one marriage or several, and she'll never notice that she loses every time. But the real value of this game is how far it distances her from the MH. The MH offers Her presence right there in her marriage, helping her to forgive, to understand, to ask for what she needs, to change where she has fallen short. Convince her that somehow her partner is an obstacle to the MH's presence instead of a way to it. Suggest to her that things would be so peaceful without him.

The MH is quite perverse, really, allowing humans to learn love via association with other unlovable humans. She seems to have specifically designed married life as a living laboratory for developing such revolting virtues as forgiveness and tolerance. Religious groups, where they are expected to practice charity toward one another, also spring to mind—and fortunately your victim attends her church too infrequently for any of their obnoxious efforts at loving-kindness to rub off.

Ψ Anesthesia

Subj: Don't count your chickens before they've hatched
From: Anasty1
To: gnawingirl

Heard all about you and Licehead and your toasts to the new couple down at Dante's. It seems that your combined wits (and a few cold ones) led you to celebrate the fact that her new husband has never had much interest in any church. You both need a cold shower, if you ask me. *She* may quit going because of him, but *he* may start going with her. Humans who have never had much exposure to a church during childhood often try it as adults, with a certain freshness you want to keep from your victim, I can assure you. Good grief, eventually *his* involvement could make *her* rethink her lackluster semiannual attendance at Christmas and Easter.

Ψ Anesthesia

Subj: No laughing matter
From: Anasty1
To: gnawingirl

Hard to believe your refusal to take this seriously. Come, now. The tour of the House of Corrections for Juvenile Incompetent Tempters is still part of your education at the Academy, I trust. You might want to review your notes on the special cell block set aside for those connected in any way with a human's beginning to go to church. *Spine tingling*, I'm sure.

Ψ Anesthesia

Subj: Now that I have your attention
From: Anasty1
To: gnawingirl

The best antidote I know is for the churchgoer to insist that the nonchurchgoer attend. If she thinks about it at all, let her think the MH wants her to nag him about it.

Ψ Anesthesia

Subj: You've only just begun
From: Anasty1
To: gnawingirl

You're taking a lot for granted these days, Termite. Just because they're married doesn't mean they're automatically done with sex. It's up to you to minimize their sexual contact, starting now, so as to build a firm basis for lasting marital disharmony.

You remember the drills. First, reverse the tactics of premarital sex. Then let her compare their sex life unfavorably to that of their early days, or to something she's seen in the movies or in books, or to some romantic notion. Let pictures of old lovers float into her mind at the most inopportune moments. Make sure that Licehead is following the same procedure with her husband. Both of you see to it that your victims are often interested in having sex, but at different times. Put it in your victim's mind that talking with her husband about sex somehow degrades the whole experience.

Make sure she never talks to the MH about her sex life; for She, in Her usual earthy way, answers these prayers under the general heading of daily bread. Sex was Her idea, after all. Her inane notion seems to be that tenderness and passion go together—or, more precisely, that the one generates the other. Couples who are happy in bed together are hard to tear apart.

Ψ Anesthesia

Subj: Completely undignified
From: Anasty1
To: gnawingirl

The fact that they derive so much enjoyment from each other's bodies is *most* unfortunate. At least *we* have enough dignity to be offended—the MH is probably smiling down at the absurd lovebirds now. But your victim doesn't know that. Convince her that her sexual behavior is shameful—somehow inappropriate, perhaps, now that she's a married woman. If she won't go that far, confuse her into thinking that the MH somehow only barely tolerates (rather than blesses) behavior which is (obviously) far more suited to the animal kingdom.

The *human* hybrid, understandably confused about the presence of both a body and a soul, can easily be led to one extreme or the other. The human as mere animal is an ugly sight; the human who loses touch with her animal nature is ugly as well. Possibly your victim might be tempted toward the latter. She might begin to think of her sex life as something she enjoyed when she was younger, sexual pleasure as something she has outgrown, etc.

Ψ Anesthesia

Subj: A prelude to more dismal days ahead
From: Anasty1
To: gnawingirl

I'm sick of watching you flounder along. Let me just tell you exactly what to do. Try encouraging her sweet tooth. If you can get her to gain another ten pounds and thus feel ashamed of her body, she may begin to pretend she no longer desires her husband, and he may begin to snipe at her. That'll put a stop to their little fun. Anything to lessen the intimacy and develop some tedium.

Ψ Anesthesia

Ψ Part Three

Subj: Just exactly what did you think would happen?
From: Anasty1
To: gnawingirl

Please. Her pregnant body and radiant appearance is bad enough—
spare me your naive sense of surprise. Not that I don't understand your
frustration: just when the ten-pound-weight-gain ploy was starting to
work, *this* had to happen. And I know that infuriating glow on her
face—reflecting the new life bursting within her, pulsating with the
energy of the universe. It's so cosmically unfair. Here we sit, unable to
create anything, having to coax the humans into becoming food for us.
And there's your human, about to give birth to yet another ridiculous
biped capable of spending eternity with the MH.

And there's the MH, always involving the humans in Her corny
plans.

Anytime a human begins to create anything, from a loaf of bread
to a symphony, the MH is there with her. Rejoicing, I'm sorry to say.
It reminds me of the stories of Creation, by all accounts a horrible
affair. All she had to do was say light, and light began happening. She
didn't even try to control it, she just let it happen. Even a hint, even
the smallest spark of that approach to life is more than we want to
allow in our victims.

Ψ Anesthesia

Subj: An endless battle
From: Anasty1
To: gnawingirl

I'm not concerned about *what* your victim might create. A trifling matter, I'm sure. I'm concerned about what happens *while* she's doing anything creative. She feels energized, possibly even happy. Whether she's
writing a symphony or planting petunias, the result, for our purposes,
is essentially the same. However temporarily, she escapes her finite
view of life and joins the MH's imagining of what might be.

Ψ Anesthesia

Subj: Time to roll up your sleeves
From: Anasty1
To: gnawingirl

Make her worry about whether she'll be a good mother, or whether she'll even like being a mother. Steer clear of any women with young babies, so that she has no chance to get comfortable. Use the same ploy that worked while she planned her wedding: ruin her happiness in the present with completely unfounded worries about the future. Train her to continue denying the MH, refusing to trust Her with her life.

Ψ Anesthesia

Subj: A Pandora's Box of human potential
From: Anasty1
To: gnawingirl

Because the MH gave the species the instinct to care for the young, chances are small that you can keep her from finding *some* satisfaction in mothering. Once she starts seeing herself as a mother, she may begin to notice other possibilities waiting to be born.

On our side, though, we do have the remarkable work of The Center for Stifling all Impulses of Creative Kinds (CSICK). That disgusting routine from earlier centuries of gathering together in the evenings to make music or to dance is almost at an end. No one sits on the front porch telling stories any more. Why, they don't even build front porches any more. Few take time to cook or ever learn to sew. Letter writing and journal keeping are both passé. Yet the humans continue to find new ways of creative expression, like e-mail and digital photos. And some traditional ways, like having children, we just haven't been able to stop.

Ψ Anesthesia

Subj: Far from new
From: Anasty1
To: gnawingirl

The revolting scene you're describing is as old as human history: your victim, rocking her baby, feeling love, and unavailable to any suggestion we might make. About all you can do in such moments is plant the expectation that she'll always feel loving in such circumstances—thus ensuring disappointment whenever she feels otherwise. Enough frustration and she'll join the parental throngs we've led to regard children *mainly* as a nuisance.

 Ψ Anesthesia

Subj: My favorite work
From: Anasty1
To: gnawingirl

The MH gives them a wonderful, priceless gift; we corrupt it into a burden. What a great time to be working out in the world! The humans have almost forgotten what's good about children. Remember when the MH's Son told the humans to let the children come, that of such was the kingdom? The humans don't even understand the story any more. They have whole sermons speculating on what it was about being a child that Her Son might have been referring to.

 Ψ Anesthesia

Subj: An either/or situation
From: Anasty1
To: gnawingirl

If you'd been keeping up with the latest trends in the Journal of Applied Methods of Alienation (JAMA), you'd already be acquainted with our strategy with regard to children, work, and community: we force women to choose among them. Either a young woman gives up her work (and her friends and community as well) to stay home alone with her baby, or she gives up her baby to the care of others so that she can continue to work all day. Compare this to a traditional village culture, or even the multigenerational farmhouse of the not-too-distant past. Women had babies, modified their work habits to care for their children, but continued to work and be a part of their community. They shared the responsibility of the children with aunts, grandmothers, sisters, friends—even, on occasion, fathers.

Ψ Anesthesia

Subj: A win/win situation
From: Anasty1
To: gnawingirl

Must I explain everything to you? She has a few months before she has to make a decision. Just get a sense of which way she is leaning and feed her the appropriate lie. If she tends to want to stay home, tell her she won't miss her work and her friends, and her baby should be all that matters anyway. If she tends to want to keep working, tell her she can get to the top in her career without depriving her child a smidgen. (Don't *go near* any way in which such a life might deprive *her*. This is one case in which self-interest is better left unevoked.) Either tack can breed enough unrealistic expectations for a lifetime of unhappiness.

Ψ Anesthesia

Subj: Habits
From: Anasty1
To: gnawingirl

Although the exercise class for new moms is not helping her to lose weight, I must remind you that it *is* making her both mentally and physically healthier. It's her habit of exercising—the discipline of it all—that you should be worrying about.

Ψ Anesthesia

Subj: Remember the era you're tempting in
From: Anasty1
To: gnawingirl

Better go back to your history books. In other times, where discipline has been in vogue, we led the humans into obstinacy and inflexibility, thereby limiting what they might create or become. But the policy of your victim's era is to discourage consistency, so that no vision has any opportunity to develop. Instant gratification has become our great ally. The gardener slogging around through a cold wet spring is considered eccentric at best, and the humans never connect her disciplined approach with her beautiful yard in the heat of the summer. The banner word, once again, is Freedom. Convince her that she is much too free to be bound to any routine and she'll never figure out how essential discipline is to true freedom.

Ψ Anesthesia

Subj: Good point
From: Anasty1
To: gnawingirl

Yes, her new baby can be relied upon to wreak havoc with her routine, at least for now. You must realize, though, that the MH also plans to use the demands of a small child to Her purposes. She intends to teach your victim to be more loving, and She will make every effort to use an infant as teacher.

Ψ Anesthesia

Subj: Sleepless nights
From: Anasty1
To: gnawingirl

Well, I don't know how you let it happen, Termite, but no matter. If she's arranged to continue to do some part-time work for her office, thus preserving both her work community and time with her baby, you'll just have to roll with it. Sounds pretty tiring, though, doesn't it?

Hmmm. Caring for two children could make it harder. How about getting her started on another right away?

Ψ Anesthesia

Subj: It could work
From: Anasty1
To: gnawingirl

Combine a lack of sleep with one new, demanding child, another on the way, and two inexperienced parents, and you have a perfect recipe for marital quarrels. Cultivate lots of anger, spoken or unspoken, for quiet seething is just as helpful as loud outbursts. The MH wishes them to turn to each other, arms outstretched, for love and support during all the difficulties of life. But humans would rather fight than admit that they need each other.

The prevailing attitude of your victim's time is that it is weak to need others. Ha! The MH's Son himself even went to the trouble of gathering and maintaining a support group, but humans think they can go it alone. Keep exalting the virtue of self-reliance; label anything else. Make her despair of the difficulty of caring for her child without ever realizing that she simply was not meant to do so apart from the rest of the human race.

Ψ Anesthesia

Subj: Feelings
From: Anasty1
To: gnawingirl

If she's starting to notice that she's overwhelmed, convince her that it's selfish to pay attention to her own feelings and needs. Equate or at least associate self-knowledge with the contemptible posture of "contemplating her navel." Take advantage of the fact that her culture values the extrovert far above the introvert. There's all the difference in the world between a human who is self-aware and a human who is self-centered, but she needn't know that!

Ψ Anesthesia

Subj: A preference for fiction
From: Anasty1
To: gnawingirl

It's the MH who wants her to know the truth about herself. We want to keep it a great secret from her. I'd go so far as to say that she's amenable to our suggestions precisely to the extent that she's kept in ignorance about herself. Anything she discovers about herself she can detach from, and we then lose manipulative leverage. Fortunately the journey of self-discovery can be quite painful, and any tempter worth her salt can keep her victim from making the trip.

Ψ Anesthesia

Subj: A typical pattern
From: Anasty1
To: gnawingirl

I wouldn't lose any sleep over it—yet. Once they have children, humans often start going to church regularly. For a while. Some sort of cultural phenomenon, totally unrelated to any newfound reliance on the MH, if that's what's on your mind. Your report is rather inadequate—I see nothing about her husband, so I'm assuming she's going alone? And what kind of a church is it? One that looks down on all who attend elsewhere, I hope. The more the humans gather to feel superior to others, the more amusement they provide once we have them here.

   Ψ Anesthesia

Subj: An old standby
From: Anasty1
To: gnawingirl

Try the standard, "I can worship on the golf course" (or in the shower or driving to work or gardening or listening to music, etc., etc.) The idea that it might be possible, or even preferable, to pray as a community does not easily occur to today's humans. Worship, they think, can be done just as well (if not better) in solitude.

   Ψ Anesthesia

Subj: Duh
From: Anasty1
To: gnawingirl

Of course the MH wants them to pray both alone *and* together. A very few of the humans, far advanced in the MH's service, have developed the ability to commune with the MH at all times, but their prayer lives are almost always rooted in an individual devotional life springing from some sort of worshiping community. They need both, Termite, it's that simple. And your victim doesn't know it. Convince her that she no longer needs her church, and you will have her halfway here.

Ψ Anesthesia

Subj: This is up to YOU
From: Anasty1
To: gnawingirl

You junior tempters always make the same mistake: blaming your advisors for your difficulties. It's not my fault if you can't break her of her new church-going habit. My job is to give advice. I can't come up there and do it for you—unlike the MH, I can't be in more than one place at a time. It is your responsibility *and yours alone* to carry out our plans. And don't come running to me every time some little ploy doesn't work. Just get busy and try something else—there's no substitute for hard work.

Until she stops going to church, you must render her time there as harmless as possible. So let her cook for the potluck, publish the newsletter, or attend endless meetings about the color scheme of the fellowship hall. In the hands of a human who might actually offer such activities as a service to the MH, this would be risky business indeed. But with an inexperienced victim, church work can easily be used to distract her from the (presumed) reason for it.

Ψ Anesthesia

Subj: The fertile field of fellowship
From: Anasty1
To: gnawingirl

I do wish you wouldn't whine. If church service isn't working, what about *fellowship*? Centuries ago, Christian fellowship meant that the humans were sharing their lives and their faith in the MH with each other. These days, it mostly means chatter. Of course there's always the small risk of real community, any time humans gather. Even the slightest sense of belonging can sometimes spell trouble. But for the most part, fellowship brings wonderful opportunities for the clever tempter. Your victim can go from gossiping ("Pray for poor Minnie, you know her daughter is running around with everything in pants . . .") to criticizing the minister ("What *was* he talking about this morning?") to lambasting the Sunday School ("Why can't they keep those children quiet?") Train your victim first to indulge in these behaviors, then to criticize them, finally to leave her church in a delightful display of hypocrisy.

Ψ Anesthesia

Subj: Any worship is too much worship
From: Anasty1
To: gnawingirl

Don't be fooled. It's a stopgap measure at best. Just because your victim is making grocery lists during worship and gossiping through the coffee hour, the MH is still capable of speaking to her at church. She's quite shameless about it, pouring out grace and wisdom at the slightest provocation. The simple physical act of worship can in itself open up the human spirit to Her. The praise that takes place in even a half-hearted worship service in itself can corrupt your victim, not to mention the true adoration that might spontaneously arise. All a human has to do to be in danger of grace is show up. That's why, sooner or later, you've got to put a stop to it

Ψ Anesthesia

Subj: Maybe you'd better take three deep breaths
From: Anasty1
To: gnawingirl

All right, you *are* in dangerous territory, but panic won't help matters. Employ the textbook method for stopping a human from reading scripture: encourage her. Tell her she should begin at the beginning and read a chapter a day. Be sure to select an appropriate translation. Maybe a study edition with multitudinous footnotes. Or one of the new ultramodern wordings, with sledgehammer lessons on every page. Or a supermodern politically correct version, with all the life sucked out of it. Anything that keeps the spirit of the MH from blowing over the Word. And make sure that she never asks Her to guide her reading. Encourage the unbelievable folly that understanding the Word would be all up to her, and then tell her to study hard.

Before you ask, let me assure you that I'm well aware of the old adage, "If they don't know what it says, they can't understand what it means." And I couldn't agree more. Study leading to comprehension is the last thing we want. What we're doing here is leading her to lose interest in the project altogether.

Ψ Anesthesia

Subj: Imagination sets in, pretty soon they're singing
From: Anasty1
To: gnawingirl

Those classic stories at the beginning can't be helped, but you can keep her from understanding them. The main thing is to limit her mind—keep her from picturing herself as Eve, for instance. A playful attitude with the stories can lead to a dangerous place beyond your control. Tell her that the study of scripture is serious business, requiring memorizing, cross-referencing, wrestling with a huge commentary, or attending to whatever dry details least appeal to her. Possibly she could *die* of boredom.

Ψ Anesthesia

Subj: Miscalculations
From: Anasty1
To: gnawingirl

Perhaps you aren't aware of my close connections to Bubonia in the Internal Records Service. She let it drop that you find my attitude regarding your victim "overly optimistic"—a reaction, no doubt, to the encouragement I indeed try to give all the junior tempters under my advisory capacity. But if you are suggesting that my optimism is unfounded or that you should not be expected to bring your victim to us, you have another think coming. I have told you from the beginning that the tempting of this "postmodern" trollop is an easy first assignment, and I'm sticking with my original assessment. Where I may have been overly optimistic is in my estimate of your abilities!

Ψ Anesthesia

Subj: Accountability
From: Anasty1
To: gnawingirl

We have a high success record to maintain, Termite—which is why we keep exhaustive records here detailing the successes and failures of every tempter. We do everything within our considerable power to convince humans they're not accountable for anything they do, but in Hell we entertain no such delusions.

Be assured that I have kept copies of all our correspondence, together with daily notes of all that you have done and not done. As you must realize, Bubonia also has documentation—and the picture it paints of you is, increasingly, *not* a pretty one. Your records are showing you to be a tempter who receives competent advice but fails to implement it. Take this information I received this morning—information I can only assume you were purposefully concealing. Your victim's husband has begun attending church with her?! Did you really think I wouldn't find out? And would he have done so had you followed my guidance? My advice was crystal clear on this topic. I ask you: what good is good advice if it is ignored?

Ψ Anesthesia

Subj: All is not lost
From: Anasty1
To: gnawingirl

Bubonia and I *can* keep a secret, Termite. The House of Corrections may not be necessary at all, and certainly makes no sense right now. If you'll get out of the IRS office and back to the daily business of guiding your victim to us, focusing your efforts as I have suggested, your success can yet be virtually guaranteed and this little matter can be quickly forgotten. There are, after all, bigger fish to fry.

Ψ Anesthesia

Subj: The right bait for your hook
From: Anasty1
To: gnawingirl

How can you take advantage of this church kick she's on, Termite? My favorite ploy goes like this: "If the one you name as Lord could bear the humiliation, betrayal, rejection, mockery, beatings, torture, and death of his last days on earth, surely you should be able to put up with _____." They miss the entire point of his sacrifice, freely offered, and get excellent training for their eternal role as victim here below. They begin to believe that the MH wants them to wake up every morning, go through the day denying themselves, and end it feeling resentful and bitter. As if the MH had given them a life to spend being treated badly, *as if that makes them holy.*

That just makes them fools, Termite, living far outside Her will. The MH's Son never let anyone use him—it's all right there in their stories about him. (And it's to our unending credit that they are so widely ignored and so reliably misunderstood.) Even in his last days, when we had him right where we wanted him, still we could not prod him into faithlessness. True to himself, true to Her, up to the end. Disgusting. I've gone over it in my mind so many times, what could we have done? Somehow we let that opportunity slip away, and just when we thought we had won: resurrection. And still the battle goes on. Next time, Termite. Tomorrow *is* another day.

But where was I? Oh yes. Self-denial. It's supposed to mean letting go of the false self, where all the pride and willfulness come into play. When a human dares to deny the false self and begins to uncover what's real, that place where her will and the MH's will become indistinguishable—well, then, Houston, we have a problem.

The MH would never want them to deny what is true—*that* has been *our* work, and very successful work indeed. So let her take on self-denial and give it a twist. It doesn't have to be anything earth-shaking, just some way to knock her off track.

Ψ Anesthesia

Subj: Back in the saddle
From: Anasty1
To: gnawingirl

Just the sort of thing I had in mind. The road to overextension is paved with self-importance—the opposite of true self-denial, but you can keep her from catching on, I trust! The world is full of humans who think they can do it all, because somebody (guess who!) made them think they *could and should*. And of course you can make her think her religion calls her to such sacrifice. At home, suggest that she is serving Her with her "helpfulness" and encourage her to be more "giving." At work, point out that the MH needs humans who are "responsible" and encourage her to be more "hard-working." You can take this one to the bank, Termite, for years, even decades, before she begins to catch on. And by then she'll have no self left to sacrifice.

Ψ Anesthesia

Subj: A mild case of martyrdom
From: Anasty1
To: gnawingirl

Let her neglect her own duties to attend to responsibilities, which indeed the MH intended for someone else. Give her the line, "If you don't do it, it won't get done." You can keep her from reading a story to her children because she is busy making phone calls about a parents' meeting at their school the next day. You can keep her from finishing her own work because she is too busy assisting a co-worker (again). Rob her of the time she needs for what the MH has given *her* to do, leaving her frustrated at the end of every day.

    Ψ Anesthesia

Subj: Helping or hurting
From: Anasty1
To: gnawingirl

You really *must* learn how to take my advice and run with it, Termite. What makes sound principles sound is their applicability to many different situations. To ruin her Sunday School class for her, make sure she teaches it alone. If she shares the teaching load she might actually start to enjoy the class, welcome an occasional break, and appreciate the camaraderie of one or more other teachers who, in turn, might learn something valuable about serving the church. Use your victim's tendency to think she's helping when she's taking all the responsibility on herself. It not only blocks the MH's work in her own life, it also blocks the MH from much creative work in other humans, who might find Her in and through their responsibilities and even their troubles. Humans who seek to take care of others often serve us rather than Her.

    Ψ Anesthesia

Subj: I'll go further
From: Anasty1
To: gnawingirl

Your victim's need to protect others from life's problems (hence lessons) is actually an expression of distrust of life. "Here, let me do that for you" can begin as a patronizing "I am afraid this will be too much for you" and culminates in a faithless "the MH won't be there for you." Eventually she will be thinking (although not consciously, of course) of herself as the savior for others. It is a grand idolatry, wherein she thinks she is serving the MH when in reality she is trying to become a god.

Ψ Anesthesia

Subj: I couldn't care less . . .
From: Anasty1
To: gnawingirl

. . . what you read in your years at the Academy. Read my h-mails and apply yourself. I'm accustomed to more professionalism, even from a new graduate. And that doctrinal gibberish you're forever quoting is absolutely useless in the real world.

Ψ Anesthesia

Subj: This is what I'm talking about
From: Anasty1
To: gnawingirl

You're missing the day-to-day opportunities. Take a load of laundry. While the MH would have her enjoying the clean, warm smell of a pair of socks as she folds them, you should be convincing her to resent every second of her labor: everything in the *&^%@$ basket is going to be dirty *again* by week's end, etc. A small thing? Not really, for a human who pays attention to such tasks or even gives thanks for them draws energy from her work. A human who performs exactly the same tasks while seething with resentment winds up feeling exhausted. The MH provides for those who choose to find Her in their lives.

Ψ Anesthesia

Subj: A light load, an easy yoke
From: Anasty1
To: gnawingirl

You keep forgetting the essential pride of the humans. They prefer heavy loads—in fact, their sense of importance requires them. The MH's Son offered them a light burden. He, like any good carpenter, could make a yoke tailored to fit an ox perfectly: no rubbing, no aching, all day long. If your victim would allow herself to be fitted for the MH's yoke, her burden would be lightened beyond her recognition. *Never, ever let her try it on.*

Ψ Anesthesia

Subj: Drop the Ox
From: Anasty1
To: gnawingirl

Have you ever played drop the ox? It's especially entertaining with the kind of human your victim is becoming. I'll treat you to a game the next time you visit.

Ψ Anesthesia

Subj: The earth version of the game
From: Anasty1
To: gnawingirl

Let's say it's her day off, and she has ten tasks planned for her morning. Then it snows and the children are home from school. Bingo, you're in business. All day long she can be fretting and fuming about how much she has to do—while remaining angry with her children and/or the weather for ruining her day. Do you see the humor of it all? "Her" day? Every moment of her life is a gift, none of it is hers. Every moment that she claims as *hers* becomes ours. If she would turn to the MH and ask for Her guidance, she might learn that the *one* small task she has to accomplish is to let go of her own plans and spend the day with her children. That's all. The yoke really *is* easy. But in order to put it on, she'd have to give up her own yoke, her claim to "her" day.

Ψ Anesthesia

Subj: Due to circumstances beyond her control
From: Anasty1
To: gnawingirl

I don't think you're getting the complete picture here. Her claim to her day is part of a wide *mural*. Her belief that she's in control of everything in the picture is the key to controlling her every move.

Here's how it works: Say she's delivering the work she did at home and if she's late *there* she'll be late getting *back*, and she's stuck in traffic. She may feel helpless, useful in developing hopelessness and despair. Or frustrated, useful in developing rage and rigidity. The only humans we don't control in heavy traffic are those few who may feel helpless or frustrated but who also know they can't do anything about the traffic flow. They've quit trying to control the world themselves and thus can *let go of* the feeling. For them the MH forms a continual backdrop, you might say, to every moment of life. And as a quick drive through any town will show, they are few and far between.

Ψ Anesthesia

Subj: Do you have no imagination whatsoever?
From: Anasty1
To: gnawingirl

Put before her a picture of what she might be getting done if not for rush hour traffic. Don't let her see that *being there* is all she has to accomplish.

Ψ Anesthesia

Subj: All the time in the world
From: Anasty1
To: gnawingirl

The MH has some very peculiar views on getting things done. Your victim waits until the children are asleep to take out the trash because they always want to help and it's more trouble for her when they do. But the MH is just the opposite. She won't act without help from a human. She could get a lot more done without them! She has an infinite patience for any human who says, like a child, "Please, I want to help." She finds some little task for her, giving all the support necessary to do what She could do in the blink of an eye. Why She would choose such an approach is incomprehensible, but also immaterial. It certainly gives us plenty of time to work!

Ψ Anesthesia

Subj: Staking a claim
From: Anasty1
To: gnawingirl

In the end, either she'll hear the MH calling and go to Her, or she'll hear us calling and come to us. And she'll come to us. We *will* claim her. Eventually we will claim all things, visible and invisible.

Ψ Anesthesia

Subj: How did you guess?
From: Anasty1
To: gnawingirl

The tempting of mothers has always been my specialty. My anti-nurturing techniques are at least as harmful to the mother as to the child, and build a firm base for an eternity of unhappiness for both.

    Ψ Anesthesia

Subj: Recent Research File Attached
From: Anasty1
To: gnawingirl

Be sure to keep the findings to yourself. Although I'm of course planning to turn in the results of my research to the lower levels, I'm not quite finished. In the meantime it does help our family to have a little edge in this area. By the way, I'm quite pleased with both your progress *and* your interest—it shows a new maturity in your work.

    Ψ Anesthesia

Ψ Part Four

Subj: Went where?!
From: Anasty1
To: gnawingirl

Sometimes humans communicate despite our best efforts. I understand that much. What I *don't* understand is how you could let her go. There, of all places. Couldn't you have convinced her that she was too tired, or too fat, or too whatever? What were you thinking?! Not about your work, that's obvious. You must take it seriously, Termite, apply yourself one hundred percent. Enough of this visiting with your old friends from college with their entertaining assignments in the prisons. Your attitude must be grim determination and total commitment.

    Ψ Anesthesia

Subj: Not funny
From: Anasty1
To: gnawingirl

If I were you I would stop laughing. You seem to think that the charismatic movement is some sort of joke, with all that arm waving and peculiar speaking. Well, it may distract her from attending her own church—but it may move her closer to the MH. You'd better pay attention, for you are in dangerous territory.

    Your victim is a prime candidate for charismania. It's always found in places and times when religion has been overly intellectualized. She's a perfect example of a human who can cite chapter and verse about the MH's love for her. But has she ever known direct experience of the MH's love? Maybe once or twice, over her whole lifetime. Charismania could change that. All their dancing and praising and singing those emotional songs you find so amusing does open up many of them to the love of the MH. I've told you before—they are *animals*. When they lift their hands to the MH, the connection between body and soul can be downright visceral.

    Ψ Anesthesia

Subj: It could work
From: Anasty1
To: gnawingirl

Your best option will be to get your victim to carry the emotional aspect of charismania to an extreme. Encourage her during these early days to count on feeling good every time she plays her silly music about the MH. Then, when a difficult time comes (as it always does) and she cannot feel Her presence on demand, weigh in on her with a feeling that she has been abandoned. Develop this element of doubt until she thinks that everything she experienced before must have been false, or just her mood, or whatever. With any luck, you might provoke a faith crisis wherein she rejects not only charismania but religion altogether. For although the MH will never leave her, your victim's sense of Her presence will come and go.

Ψ Anesthesia

Subj: Surprise, surprise
From: Anasty1
To: gnawingirl

The fact that the MH sometimes provides sweet consolations to those who truly turn to Her, and sometimes withholds them, is not news to *us*. But it would be to her. You and I know that mystical Christians (another pesky group with a sense of the MH's love for the humans) have for centuries written about the dark night of the soul, and so on. Fortunately, such writings are far removed from the world of your victim's new acquaintances. Your victim will have no idea that she might have expected the time to come when she would feel nothing.

Ψ Anesthesia

Subj: I know just the thing
From: Anasty 1
To: gnawingirl

Consider the tendency of the charismaniacs to think of themselves as powerful. My hat's off to our Heresy Division for managing such an astonishing line of thought. They can actually worship the one who died on a cross in the most outrageous act of powerlessness the world has ever known—and still think the MH wants them to be powerful. Brilliant! Not only many charismaniacs but in fact most humans in general—going all the way back to the beginning—prefer a powerful god, a god in control, a god they can count on to bring happiness, safety, prosperity. Some actually teach that if a human prays hard enough their prayers will be answered: the "name it and claim it" approach. If they think to add "thy will be done," it is with the thought that of course they already know the MH's will on every conceivable subject.

    Ψ Anesthesia

Subj: Here's a possible opening
From: Anasty 1
To: gnawingirl

Doesn't one of your victim's children have asthma? Every time she starts wheezing, have her put her hands on her child and demand the MH's healing power in a forceful, powerful voice. Obviously it is Her will, right? An appeal to the MH as Magician will *guarantee* her failing to see the cross for what it represents: the MH's choice to be with them in their pain, not avoid it.

    Ψ Anesthesia

Subj: What do you take me for, a fortune teller?
From: Anasty1
To: gnawingirl

I don't know whether She will get rid of the asthma. Even our most experienced experts can't predict that. She's always working to heal, but a cure is a different story. My guess is that She might use the asthma to promote a sense of compassion for others in the little brat, but we just can't be sure. I do know this: She's not big on performing miracles for an audience. Most of Her healing goes on when no one is looking. She's rumored to *begin* the healing of some of their deepest wounds only after their entrance to the next life. Who knows, Termite? She's so utterly capricious it's a wonder that any of the humans will have anything to do with Her.

Ψ Anesthesia

Subj: Spare us the political games
From: Anasty1
To: gnawingirl

Feeling oh-so-clever, are we? It doesn't take genius to have downloaded my file on parenting tips and paraded it around the lower levels. Regarding the little issue you raised about whether I was holding back my findings for my own use, all that has been taken care of through a colleague in Research and Development. I simply explained that I was polishing my paper before presenting it, and of course she understood. She now has the finished product on her desk. Your unfortunate display of bravado will get you nowhere, Termite. If you want accolades from below, bring us your victim.

Ψ Anesthesia

Subj: A real chance to bring her down
From: Anasty1
To: gnawingirl

It's not spectacular, but so much the better. While the MH would have her be concerned for *all* the boys trying out, we can so easily suggest that it is somehow more important for *hers* to win. We can lead your victim to see life as made up of winners and losers, Termite. Nothing could be better for our purposes, except its corollary: the desire to make herself and her family the winners.

    Ψ Anesthesia

Subj: Abundant foolishness
From: Anasty1
To: gnawingirl

Finally we get to place your victim squarely on our turf, facing our reality. We recognize the world as a place of conquest and defeat. It is a war we will obviously win, for the MH's absurd notion of an abundant life is simply unfathomable. She wants them to believe that there is enough for everyone. Enough what? Enough of Her, enough of what Her Son called living water and claimed that those who have it will never thirst. Ha! Tell that to a human on a hot day.

    Ψ Anesthesia

Subj: Beyond all reason
From: Anasty1
To: gnawingirl

Yes, it does sound as if I'm saying that the MH loves them. But how *could* She love the fools, much less love them individually and infinitely? Why *would* She bother? All of our studies have failed to reveal to us Her true purpose. Although we don't know what She is really up to, we do know that it is essential to keep this idea of the abundant life from the humans.

Our view, firmly established on earth, is one of scarcity. There are only fifteen slots on the ball team, Termite. Don't let her forget it. There's not *enough* for everyone.

Ψ Anesthesia

Subj: A traditional strategy, tried and true
From: Anasty1
To: gnawingirl

Scarcity is the doctrinal basis for two of our most important tempting tools: competition and its cousin, gluttony. The word "gluttony" is so positively *medieval* that most humans are blind to its influence. (And kudos to our Linguistics Department for the convenient label.) Don't make the mistake of assuming that gluttony simply involves tempting her to compete with her neighbors for a fancier car or a nicer house or a more exotic vacation. Although financial troubles and the nuisance of overconsumption do serve to distract humans from the MH, we can have much more.

Ψ Anesthesia

Subj: A Tempter's Delight
From: Anasty1
To: gnawingirl

What we really want out of gluttony is idolatry. The false god of a place for her kid on the ball team today, a parking spot with her name on it at work tomorrow, and who knows what the next day. . . . Daily, consistent training for your victim that if she only had x (or y or z), she would be satisfied. Her whole self groans for the MH, like an empty stomach rumbles for food, but she is completely unaware of the way to fullness. Gluttony, my dear, is a never-ending source of possibilities.

Ψ Anesthesia

Subj: The three-thonged approach to gluttony
From: Anasty1
To: gnawingirl

We had to memorize these back when I was at the Academy:
- *Appeal to her pride: the more she has, the more puffed up she becomes.*
- *Speak to her fears: the more she has, the more she fears that all may be taken from her.*
- *Nurture her need to be powerful: the more she has, the more she can control others.*
  Ψ Anesthesia

Subj: I smell something fishy
From: Anasty1
To: gnawingirl

For once, Termite, you are not to blame. What you've got here is a certifiable case of the MH's meddling—it's got *Her* written all over it. Your victim's son is hugely disappointed when he doesn't make the school team. Then his dad, who's never made time before, signs up to coach the recreational league. So father and son have this great spring playing and talking baseball instead of the son sitting miserably on the school team bench all season. How typical. She's always taking a bad situation and making it better than originally planned. I must admit that even I have on occasion seen my finest efforts undone.
Ψ Anesthesia

Subj: No boundaries for Her
From: Anasty1
To: gnawingirl

The work of the MH, haphazard as it may be, spills over. She can't quit with letting the kid play ball. Oh, no. Now your victim sees her husband in a new light and is feeling a new tenderness toward him. Moreover, she's returned to her former church, not over some petty disenchantment with the charismaniacs, but with new insight. She has realized that all her prayers (demands) that her son make the team were an attempt to use the MH as a sort of magic wand waved over their lives. All she's told her minister is that the charismatic church wasn't for her, but deep down I fear that she may actually have learned something. The MH is on a roll, Termite. You've got to stop Her.

    Ψ Anesthesia

Subj: Damage Control
From: Anasty1
To: gnawingirl

The good news is that your victim hasn't made the final, crucial connection: that the MH is at the bottom of all this. She doesn't seem to be relating her own circumstances to (excuse the expression) "plenteous redemption." She's walking around reeking with life-is-good perfume, but she hasn't thought to give thanks to the Author of Life. Any damage from this little incident can be fleeting—*if* you can keep her from noticing the MH's hand in it.

    Ψ Anesthesia

Subj: An attitude without gratitude
From: Anasty1
To: gnawingirl

No, she's not going to notice the obvious. She's a human being, remember? All you have to do is distract her for a little while, until this whole thing blows over. Once a new problem arises, she'll never look back thankfully—especially if she's not remembering to thank the MH now.
   Ψ Anesthesia

Subj: Like taking candy from a baby
From: Anasty1
To: gnawingirl

Just keep her watching television, or baking brownies, or on the telephone, or finishing that one file for work, whatever, until it's too late to *think* about any devotional time.
   Ψ Anesthesia

Subj: An unlikely ally
From: Anasty1
To: gnawingirl

Don't forget the Church! In the battle to keep your victim too busy to notice the MH, enlist the Church itself, which has accepted—almost without a murmur—the current cultural assumption that more is always better. The current list of Church-sponsored programs, activities, events, meetings, and lectures can overwhelm even our best-trained workaholics—a schedule filled to overflowing like a trash can on garbage day.

   I find particularly amusing the Lenten discipline now being encouraged: taking something on, rather than giving something up. Not that we desire the projects suggested. But the Church has lost sight of the reason it used to call her members to give something up for Lent: the conscious effort to deny oneself in some exterior fashion models a process in the human's interior life. If a human is to find her true center, where she and the MH may become one, she must first give up everything that's blocking her way to that center.

Ψ Anesthesia

Subj: This may come as a surprise
From: Anasty1
To: gnawingirl

Your victim has *no idea*—no awareness whatsoever—of the MH within. How could she miss it? Well, beyond the fact that she's too busy to notice, the Church doesn't tell her to look. Oh, the Church used to teach both the inner dwelling of the MH and the way inside that "interior castle," as one of their wretched writers called it back in medieval times. But only scholars and nuns read that stuff any more.

Ψ Anesthesia

Subj: What else?
From: Anasty1
To: gnawingirl

Prayer, Termite, is the only way into the castle. It's incredible what I have to explain to you. I can only hope your victim is equally clueless.

Ψ Anesthesia

Subj: That's a big IF
From: Anasty1
To: gnawingirl

If your victim thinks at all about prayer, she probably thinks that she must work at it, develop skills, become good at it. Keep her busy thinking of what she should say to the MH, and how she should say it—as though praying were mainly up to her—and she may never hear Her. But if your victim ever begins to pray with the smallest recognition of what she is really doing and how little she can comprehend of Who she is praying to—if she ever tries to empty herself of all her preconceived ideas of the MH and asks Her to reveal Herself *as She truly is*—then the game is, at least for the moment, up.

Prayer is best kept on that wonderful list of things that your human wants to do but never quite gets around to.

Ψ Anesthesia

Subj: Busy as a beaver
From: Anasty1
To: gnawingirl

Try a pep talk about the need to be more productive, or even the need to do more for the MH. If the commandment about keeping the Sabbath should occur to her, remind her that it's not important because it's from their Old Testament—an ancient heresy, tried and true. Keep her a slave to activity, seven days a week. Convince her that she's certainly not in need of something as simple as rest, that it's wrong to do *nothing*. Encourage a gluttonous appetite to do more and more. Her society sees busyness as admirable, very busy people as morally superior—to the point that most humans feel guilty when they're *not* busy. Just chime in.

Ψ Anesthesia

Subj: A lack of humility that's good for business
From: Anasty1
To: gnawingirl

Of course my suggestion is orthodox—too subtle for your narrow mind, perhaps, but entirely orthodox. In convincing her that she can fit more into a day than is possible, you are following the standard throw-yourself-from-the-pinnacle-of-the-temple line. Your victim *wants* to believe that she can live beyond the laws of space and time in her world. Keep her thinking that she's more than human, and someday we'll show her how very human she was.

    Ψ Anesthesia

Subj: The finer points
From: Anasty1
To: gnawingirl

A vacation is fine—but while she's at the beach she might as well be catching up on a few files from the office. Encourage her to cook while she's on the telephone, make lists while she's watching an old movie, pay bills in a few spare minutes at work, and so on. . . . Enough of this and the pleasure in cooking, old movies, children, or life in general has disappeared into the multi-tasking hopper. And more than that—the contemplative dimension of any activity is avoided. *Never allow her the luxury of thinking about what she is doing.*

    Ψ Anesthesia

Subj: Trouble in River City
From: Anasty1
To: gnawingirl

I know I told you to increase her activities. And I realize I advised you earlier that "fellowship" might develop into many hours of superficial, trivial, gossipy conversation. But a small group where they talk about their lives and relate their stories to the scriptures is *not* what I had in mind.

It doesn't take a genius, Termite, to grasp that a main element of our attack on your victim was simply to keep her lonely—busy, but lonely. Just because she stayed busy didn't mean she was *connecting* with all those humans she saw every day. She was too caught up in succeeding (and making sure that her children succeeded) to have any real time for anyone else. Until now. With these friends you've allowed her, who knows what she may make time for.

Ψ Anesthesia

Subj: You have a problem
From: Anasty1
To: gnawingirl

Humans getting together to go hear a lecture would be bad enough, but friends gathering to share and to pray is disaster! In a small group in prayer, the MH's presence is going to be so obvious that even your thick-headed victim can't miss Her. Worst of all, her private devotional life may be enhanced by some mysterious connection to time spent in prayer with others.

Ψ Anesthesia

Subj: Stop it. Now.
From: Anasty1
To: gnawingirl

It's not *all* so mysterious, Termite. It's pretty obvious that she's learning from her new friends. Learning about community. About real prayer. Surely you don't think she spontaneously started picturing health for her sick friend? Someone has *taught* her to go beyond mere words to a more open imagining of what might be.

It's time to stop these lessons. Do your part to keep them chatting until the last minute, so that the prayer time is brief and superficial. This should be fairly easy to manage, as all humans are at least partly resistant to prayer anyhow. I must warn you, however, that once they get started the MH will protect them, making it difficult if not impossible for you to interrupt their worship time.

Ψ Anesthesia

Subj: What a wimp!
From: Anasty1
To: gnawingirl

One brief encounter—and not that they aren't painful, believe me, I've been there—but one short moment with the brightness of the MH and you rush away, leaving your victim vulnerable to a lesson on how to hear the MH in scripture. How to picture herself in the stories, of all things. You should have stayed to do battle. Brought the material back to intellectual ground, where you at least have a fighting chance to distract her. Now that she's learned that study is a *preface* to praying with scripture, you have a regular nightmare on your hands.

Ψ Anesthesia

Subj: Enough!
From: Anasty1
To: gnawingirl

You and the other tempters involved in allowing this mess had better start cleaning it up. Try taking advantage of a general confusion about the nature of community—a natural discomfort with conflict, or anything negative—or anything, for that matter, passionate. They are women, after all, in a time and place where women are supposed to be *nice*. Try encouraging a belief that any unpleasantness threatens the group. (Eventually such a group will die a slow and lingering death.) Incite the formation of little gossiping subgroups, in which case you and the other tempters can finish off another futile effort at human togetherness.

Ψ Anesthesia

Subj: Gossip is a subtle art
From: Anasty1
To: gnawingirl

Start with something minor and work your way up. Let your victim go home and complain to her husband about Mary coming late—again— and they have to fill her in on everything, which wastes their precious time. He's been well trained not to bother to listen to her, so then she might call another group member, just to chat, you see. . . . But never let them bring it up in the group, in front of Mary. Oh no, that would be rude, you see, too direct, and definitely not *nice*. Keep the focus on being nice, and you'll never have to worry about their telling the truth. If they tell the truth, the group might survive and even flourish. With truth comes knowledge of the MH, compassion for each other, intimacy, and even energy. Truth! It's our greatest enemy, next to the MH Herself.

Ψ Anesthesia

Subj: You've done it again!
From: Anasty1
To: gnawingirl

Let me make sure I've got this straight. An older woman in the group has talked with them all about being more open with each other. Your victim has spent the week barely smiling, rarely talking, thinking over her behavior. And you're thrilled to report her newfound misery.

I know the word "repentance" is rarely used on earth any more, but I would have thought that a tempter trained in our schools—from our family, no less—would have recognized it when she saw it. It doesn't matter now exactly who started it, or exactly what happened. Once a human begins to repent, we're up against the honesty that someone dared to begin. *They* start to be honest with each other, *we* lose control.

Still thrilled?

Ψ Anesthesia

Subj: Not my problem
From: Anasty1
To: gnawingirl

It's perverse, I must agree, the type She selects for Her work. Often her prize candidate will be an older human without a shred of dignity who has done the miserable work of looking honestly at her own pathetic life. People like that can see the sin but love the sinner—in their own person, or in another, they lose all perspective. But if you think you're getting any sympathy from me or anyone on your review panel, think again. If you want to know how this happened, look in the mirror.

Ψ Anesthesia

Subj: Pay attention
From: Anasty1
To: gnawingirl

Stop trying to avoid the problem and listen to your aunt for a change. The road of repentance begins where your victim is *right now*, taking an honest look inward. Next, she might see her sin and (with the help of the MH) might turn and go in another direction. She might actually, sincerely, apologize to her friends. If she experiences forgiveness, expect her to become more forgiving—which slams the door on many opportunities for developing the resentment, hostility, and bitterness that have occasioned such piddling success as you have enjoyed up until now. Who knows, she could become one of those open, caring types who aren't threatened by anything another says and can be *relied upon* to tie us in knots.

She may, while she is on this inner exploration, find other areas that she would just as soon leave behind, areas where she realizes that she is living outside of what the MH would have her become. As she repents of what is false in her and her life, she will become not only what is true to the MH but also what is true to herself.

These, Termite, are fruits of repentance. *Wake up.*

Ψ Anesthesia

Subj: Fruit of repentance II
From: Anasty1
To: gnawingirl

Her newfound ability to see the humor in everything (especially in herself) can be traced straight back to her penitential posturing. *She's getting loose!* And it's going to get worse. It's going to get harder and harder to entice her to continue doing anything once she's confessed it. The next time you tempt her to lord it over her children, or treat her husband with disdain, she may notice her behavior, repent, and go another way. And once a human gets into the wretched habit of repenting, she becomes much more forgiving of others. Mark my words, around the corner for your victim lies peace within and harmony with others.

Are you beginning to get the picture?

Ψ Anesthesia

Subj: Finally, you're asking the right question
From: Anasty1
To: gnawingirl

First, if it's not too late, try convincing her that she had nothing to confess, she was just misunderstood. No human ever wants to admit anything was her fault, so she may be very willing to follow your suggestion here. Next, stir up in her a sense of having been wronged. Surely someone in the group never liked her anyhow? Suggest it, true or not. Or so-and-so treated her badly or unfairly? This is likely to have some basis in reality—after all, the group is just a bunch of humans, I'm sure someone bumbled something, somehow. Get her to pout over what happened, to obsess about the person who was really at fault. Make her swear that while she may stay in the group, she will never open herself up to intimate friendships again. A lifetime of damage can result.

Ψ Anesthesia

Subj: Afterthought
From: Anasty1
To: gnawingirl

Certainly convince her, once these seeds have sprouted, to leave the group. Possibly the whole group will come to pieces over her. But that benefit is down the road. The main thing is to turn this penitent behavior around. Restore her sense of pride in her own virtue. Get her focused on whatever sin you can help her to find in her group, rather than the sin in her own heart.

Ψ Anesthesia

Subj: The MH is probably laughing at us right now
From: Anasty1
To: gnawingirl

So far we've been outmaneuvered in that little group, that's all there is to it. You'll have to get them off the scriptures. How about getting your victim to propose a self-help book for them to study next? The phrase "self-help" is in itself so nicely reminiscent of the absurd American notion of the "self-made" man or woman. Although they have everything to be thankful for, their hearts are cold with the certainty that they have *earned* it alone. To turn to another human and say thanks would be a sign of failure, or inadequacy, or dependence. To say thank you to the MH would be all of the above. Some careful work along these lines *may* enable you to convince your victim that she can manage alone. (Never mind that she's reading the book with a group, she won't see the lack of logic.)
    Ψ Anesthesia

Subj: The rumor you heard is partly true
From: Anasty1
To: gnawingirl

I only wrote the refrain for the song, "I did it my way." But it's a classic, I must admit.
    Ψ Anesthesia

Subj: You won't break that habit overnight
From: Anasty1
To: gnawingirl

Face it, those deluded group members are likely to relate *anything* to the MH. But some titles lend themselves to our work better than others. Look for texts that will get them to focus outside themselves, on plans or strategies or resolutions. (Texts that can be used again later to make her feel like a failure.) Stay away from anything that encourages inner discovery. Avoid like the plague any title that begins by proclaiming human "powerlessness."

Ψ Anesthesia

Subj: What's so bad about it?!
From: Anasty1
To: gnawingirl

I'll tell you what's so bad about it. Your victim's grandparents on the farm were familiar with powerlessness—between bad weather and sickness among the livestock, it was only too clear. But your victim nurtures the illusion that she is in charge of her world. Although she may appeal to the MH in some special circumstance, in general she still thinks she has things pretty well under control. Praying for her daily bread, learning to rely each moment on a strength greater than her own—these habits are unnatural to her. Unnatural = uncomfortable = . . . I don't know, untenable, unworthy, unhappy, whatever fits. Get this kind of equation going and she's unlikely to stick with the behavior long enough to find out what it's really setting in motion.

Ψ Anesthesia

Subj: This is more like it
From: Anasty1
To: gnawingirl

As long as she's reading something with tedious sentences about "appropriately assertive anger" or "great gainable goals," she isn't going to get lost in one of those good mystery novels she used to enjoy. Take the fun out of her life, I like that.

Ψ Anesthesia

Subj: A balancing act
From: Anasty1
To: gnawingirl

Be careful not to go too far, Termite. Remember your history lessons, and the unfortunate examples of promising humans who were set free from the need to be perfect precisely insofar as we were tempting them to despair of their imperfections. Your victim could also wake up to grace.

    Ψ Anesthesia

Subj: Dangerous Business
From: Anasty1
To: gnawingirl

Yes, your job (at least for the moment) lacks glamour. Your friends with assignments in the prisons do get to see some pretty sights on a regular basis. But if you think their work is easy, you are mistaken. Have you noticed the real, praying communities some of those humans have created? And have you heard the prayers coming from those places? They pray for their *captors*—how can we control people like that? And who knows whether the MH might not honor their grotesque prayers? Stay out of those places, they aren't safe! The humans there are only too aware that they aren't in control—why, some have even considered their own mortality. Your victim lives in a much safer little place for our purposes, a place where no human ever stops to think that she might, someday, die.

    Ψ Anesthesia

Subj: A break
From: Anasty1
To: gnawingirl

Finally, that obnoxious small group will become a thing of the past. Make sure the movers pack that pernicious prayerbook so far down in the box that she never finds it again.

Ψ Anesthesia

Ψ Part Five

Subj: A no-brainer
From: Anasty1
To: gnawingirl

You've got it backwards. It's fine for her to move close to her in-laws. It might even be fun, stirring up a little competition between her and them for her husband's (ever-diminishing) attention. A move back to her own family, now that might be a problem. She still sees things through the lens of her childhood—and that's a far cry from the way the MH would have her look at life. Let her spend enough time around her family and she might begin to recognize the truth of it all. She might realize that her sharp tongue has been *generations* in the making. Surely you didn't think you deserved the credit for it?

Yet again I find myself explaining basic aspects of her world that you should have learned at the Academy. But I'll deal with you later. Right now we must get to the business at hand.

Ψ Anesthesia

Subj: Sunday shopping
From: Anasty1
To: gnawingirl

If you can't keep her from looking around for a new church near her new home, at least make sure she treats her Sunday mornings like shopping trips. Keep her too busy comparing the advantages and disadvantages of each place to even think about worshiping the MH while she's there.

Ψ Anesthesia

Subj: We're in the money
From: Anasty1
To: gnawingirl

With her husband going off to his demanding new job and her children in school, she's right where you want her—alone and lonely for much of the day. Once she gets sufficiently depressed about it all, she won't have the energy to find work, or any friends. Perhaps she can go on an eating binge, and then get more depressed. Many possibilities!

Ψ Anesthesia

Subj: No more tears!
From: Anasty1
To: gnawingirl

No, no, no! Don't let her grieve about her old home, her old friends, her old job. The MH would be with her in that. This is critical, Termite: the MH takes care of anyone who turns to Her in poverty of spirit. She doesn't deliver a human from her sorrow, that's not Her way. *She stays with her in it!*

It's a situation easily remedied. Tell her that she's being faithless to the MH when she misses her former home and encourage her to try harder to act like everything's fine. Convince her that "thy will be done" means she has to be happy about whatever happens to her. That's just close enough to the truth to confuse her thoroughly.

Ψ Anesthesia

Subj: Good news/bad news
From: Anasty1
To: gnawingirl

It's obvious to us that what they call the Good News includes no guarantees about how life will go for the believer. In fact it contains some stunningly clear examples that it may go very poorly by human standards. But she'll never catch on. Tempters working at a level of security clearance even lower than mine have planted in the human mind the notion that every happy, prosperous human has divine connections, and that every down-and-out human has been abandoned by the MH. Even her Son's rather graphic example of the difference between feeling forsaken and being forsaken hasn't shaken this elegantly insidious falsehood out of many human heads.

Ψ Anesthesia

Subj: Phase two
From: Anasty1
To: gnawingirl

Now that she's been feeling low for a while, it's time to begin the next phase of your attack. Suggest to her that her continued difficulties show her faith to have been futile. Don't bother trying to get her to question the existence of a deity—that wouldn't work with her at this point, and it's not necessary anyway. Just get her to wondering if her faith in a God who cares about her (i.e. the MH) wasn't just residual immaturity, her present dissatisfaction evidence that she's outgrowing it. Encourage her to view what she experienced in her small group as a fluke, or a phase, or a fantasy, and her time alone now as somehow more real. Should this thought prove dismaying, remind her to rely on the one sure avenue of help: her own resources. Chances are she'll forget all about hope as the essential character of her faith (and no one ever hears a sermon about it anymore).

Ψ Anesthesia

Subj: Hopelessly confused
From: Anasty1
To: gnawingirl

It just makes your job a little harder, not impossible. If she's settled on the notion that she must have hope, you make sure she confuses hope with expectations. Let her expectations become demands for how life should go. Set her up with false hopes, then beat her down with circumstances. It's a traditional recipe for despair, and the MH will be nowhere in sight. Hoping in Her requires a human to let go of her own expectations for how things will go.

Ψ Anesthesia

Subj: Six of one . . .
From: Anasty1
To: gnawingirl

. . . half a dozen of another. It's not surprising that she and her husband are having . . . marital problems, as they say. Who would want to come home to the frustrated, depressed old hag she's becoming? That's the last thing he wants to deal with at the end of the day. But whether they choose a bitter divorce or stay in an increasingly unhappy marriage is immaterial. Either way, she's coming our way. Because there's always the possibility that a formal separation could wake them both up to their true situation, I'd let it alone, Termite, at least for now.

Ψ Anesthesia

Subj: No big deal
From: Anasty1
To: gnawingirl

So what. Let her go to a physician's office for her depression. With any luck at all the doctor will immediately prescribe a nice antidepressant. If she needed the medicine, your job would be to keep her away from it. But your victim needs to experience her sadness, and if she lightens her mood through medication she may never deal with it. This happy turn of events could become a most welcome habit. Develop a situation where grief, sadness, and every dark feeling routinely end up buried within, haunting her without her knowing it, keeping her from ever returning to any real faith in the MH.

     Ψ Anesthesia

Subj: How predictable
From: Anasty1
To: gnawingirl

So the doctor suggested counseling. What a surprise. You'll probably want to have her avoid it. Although sometimes we can use it to confuse a human, in other cases it nurtures a most unfortunate clarity. You might suggest that she can't afford it, what with the move and all. Or appeal to her sense of pride (counseling is for the weak, etc.). Or maybe she will be just too depressed to go that day.

     Ψ Anesthesia

Subj: Good, but not good enough
From: Anasty1
To: gnawingirl

I can hardly believe your report that she's taking her dog for a walk every day because their new home doesn't have a fenced-in yard. How could you fail to foresee what would happen? Fresh air, sunshine, walking, the dog romping—how *could* you let her go? And how typical of the MH to use a *dog*. She can be counted upon to reach out to these creatures in the most undignified of ways.

It *was* a neat trick, hiding her prayer book in a box of books that would not be unpacked until she painted the study, then ensuring that her depression kept her from getting around to it. But now that she's come in from her walk sufficiently energized to begin the painting, that little game is up. Any new ideas?

Ψ Anesthesia

Subj: Oh, come on!
From: Anasty1
To: gnawingirl

She gathered up her energy to go on a retreat sponsored by her new church, told another human all about her troubles—and not just any human, but an elderly human known by us to be far advanced in the MH's service—and *then* you lost control?!?!? No, my dear, you lost control when you allowed her to share her thoughts and feelings. And, more basically, when you let her settle on a particular church and go on such a trip.

And when you let her walk that *@#^%%** dog.

Ψ Anesthesia

Subj: Another elementary error
From: Anasty1
To: gnawingirl

Watching her spill her guts may have been amusing, but if you thought it would bring on another wave of depression you were sadly mistaken. If she had to talk, you could have at least seen that she blabbed to someone who would get busy giving advice, minimizing the problem, or changing the subject. Once a human is allowed the privilege of sharing with a person who is actually listening, the MH is quickly at work. Now your victim is set up to let her troubles go and move on in her life. Worse than that, she's started looking to the MH again.

   Ψ Anesthesia

Subj: Square one
From: Anasty1
To: gnawingirl

Actually you're much further back than square one. Once a victim starts recognizing her absolute dependence on the MH—once the MH has become more than an emergency back-up to her own system— you're in for a serious battle. That recognition of the MH's love for her and the (however small) beginnings of a real love in return are potentially disastrous.

   Of course the sweet consolations of prayer will come and go, but I doubt that your victim will be fooled again into thinking that the MH is absent simply because she cannot feel Her presence. Instead of outgrowing her faith, I'm afraid she may have outgrown acting as though she was born again yesterday.

   Ψ Anesthesia

Subj: Oh gag! Bring her to me, I'll feed her something.
From: Anasty1
To: gnawingirl

Take her romantic longing to be "spiritually fed" at church and twist it. Let her go each week with some expectation of what she should be spiritually fed and how it might feel to be full. It's child's play to help her to interpret her actual experience as falling short of this ideal.

Ψ Anesthesia

Subj: Planting doubt
From: Anasty1
To: gnawingirl

Yes, yes, her new church is fine, delightful . . . you can let her think all that. Just start asking her if *her* needs are being met. Eventually you may be able to convince her to skip worship altogether, on the grounds that she's "not getting that much out of it." I assure you, I have used this trick a thousand times. Most of the humans of the Western world lack the most basic concept of worship as their central, communal act of loving, thanking, and praising the MH. They really think they are there for some sort of self-improvement.

Ψ Anesthesia

Subj: Did you flunk world history?
From: Anasty1
To: gnawingirl

Because, Termite, what we have managed to do with their culture really has been the work of a genius. Raised on the notion of success, they apply it to religion and actually attend church in order to "better" themselves. A wonderfully subtle form of idolatry develops that can be quite useful in keeping their minds closed to the MH.

I know, I know, the one they profess as Lord showed, in his own life and death, a singular lack of concern for success by human standards. Just be sure to distract her if this point is ever made at church! Keep her focused on improving herself. If she begins to think about the MH, turn her attention to thinking about whether she has or hasn't succeeded in pleasing Her. As long as her mind is bent on herself, she can go to church forever without worshiping.

Ψ Anesthesia

Subj: Don't go there
From: Anasty1
To: gnawingirl

True worship is, of course, to be avoided at all costs. How *did* you let her find her way to a community gathered for the wretched purposes of realizing the presence of the MH in the world? And of course they don't stop there, they go on to invite Her to enter the world more fully through the offering of themselves. *Another disaster looms!*

Ψ Anesthesia

Subj: Distasteful topics
From: Anasty1
To: gnawingirl

As for their Lord's Supper, that truly repulsive rite sometimes called Holy Communion (or Mass, or Eucharist, or whatever), *don't get me started*. About the slander that we flee worship out of fear lest *we* be sucked into such foolishness: obviously we don't flee. We simply remove ourselves an infinite distance—not out of fear but for the excellent reason that to witness such absurdities would be an affront to our dignity. My advice to you is to do the same.

Ψ Anesthesia

Subj: Let the record reflect . . .
From: Anasty1
To: gnawingirl

. . . that my advice has been of its usual top quality. However, it does paint an increasingly dismal picture as to your efforts, Termite. Are you sure your heart is in your work?

Ψ Anesthesia

Subj: Bungled from the beginning, but never mind
From: Anasty1
To: gnawingirl

Here's what's going to save *your* bacon: She's just a human, after all, and over time she may become amenable to your suggestions once again. With hard work and persistence on your part, she could forget her brief dance with the MH. If she lives to the average age of a human in her world, you have twenty, thirty, maybe forty or more years to bring her back our way.

Ψ Anesthesia

Subj: Finally, some good news
From: Anasty1
To: gnawingirl

For now, you just whisper to her that this little lump is probably nothing. And Termite, way to be paying attention for once in her life. What a *charming* turn of events. Let's just see how far her little faith in the MH gets her now.

Ψ Anesthesia

Subj: Standard Operating Procedure
From: Anasty 1
To: gnawingirl

Shocking that you would even ask such a question. Surely you remember your oath to promote falsehood. You *must* lead her to deny the signs that something's wrong. I appreciate your concern that if it's allowed to grow and spread long enough it may shorten her life, giving you less time to work on her. But don't you see that time might no longer matter? Really, Termite, it's time for you to catch on to the game plan here.

The game is to train her to avoid reality. Reality—that's where the MH is to be found. True religion teaches a human to trust the MH with the way things really are. Your job is to train yours to prefer what is false—trusting us, though of course she'll have no idea that this is what she's doing—any more than she'll know she's stopped following the MH. Pull this off and we can all stop worrying about the location of her future, eternal home.

Ψ Anesthesia

Subj: It had to happen
From: Anasty 1
To: gnawingirl

It's understandable of course. You couldn't wait to terrorize her—five minutes after she's diagnosed, you have to go and help her picture herself after a few chemotherapy treatments, bald head and all, then watch her fall to pieces as you nurture the fear fantasy of an agonizingly slow, excruciatingly painful death.

Enough, already. For Hell's sake, Termite, you don't want her to think about her own dying. Her prognosis may be just the ticket for us, but only if it's handled with *care*. Easy does it, now—bring her down on the sleepy wide way.

Ψ Anesthesia

Subj: Maybe, maybe not
From: Anasty1
To: gnawingirl

She may survive this time, she may not. What is certain is that she'll die sometime, and that's the astoundingly simple bit of information that is never discussed in her culture. Convince her that she must "keep her chin up and fight this thing," implying that she must never allow herself to consciously consider, much less mention, the possibility that she might actually be a mortal-by-definition human whose life is now coming to an end. Licehead must encourage her husband to deny the obvious as well. Keep her from anything *real*, Termite, from anything that might wake her up to her ultimate . . . shall we say *conclusion*?
    Ψ Anesthesia

Subj: A gold mine
From: Anasty1
To: gnawingirl

Cancer "treatment"?! Why, I've been in medieval torture chambers that seem mild in comparison. But although treatment may be fun to watch, it's neither panacea nor plague in itself. And although it may be a given that she'll choose treatment—most of the humans do, at least at first—what's important is *why*.
    Ψ Anesthesia

Subj: Why
From: Anasty1
To: gnawingirl

Now pay attention Termite, for it took me a long time and a lot of trial and error to learn this one. Motive is crucial to decisions about cancer treatment. If your victim chooses treatment out of a true desire to continue living for some purpose greater than the continuation of herself on earth, then we're in real trouble. But if she chooses treatment only out of a fear of dying, she is all but ours. (And the terror of the months or years that remain to her can be delightful.)

On the other hand, should she *refuse* treatment out of awareness that all of her living, including her death, is blessed by the MH—we have little chance of victory. But should she choose to refuse treatment out of a general sense of despair over the meaningless of her existence, well, perhaps soon we will be welcoming her to that realm in which we give new meaning to the word despair.

Ψ Anesthesia

Subj: Opportunity is knocking and you're not listening
From: Anasty1
To: gnawingirl

It's to your *advantage* that cancer therapy is so uncertain. She can go to three different doctors and get three different opinions on how to proceed—not because they're trying to confuse her but simply because no one really knows for sure what is best. Add to that the fiendishly complex bureaucracy for medical care in her country, which ensures that she will spend untold hours trying to decide what to do and untold more figuring out who might pay for what. . . . But in the end she will have to opt for some course of action—refusing treatment is an action too, even as not deciding is in itself a decision.

The trick is to keep her rethinking her choices. Does she know all she needs to know? Are her doctors to be trusted? One minute she might be firm in her resolve to follow plan A. The next minute you can have her sitting in a chair receiving chemotherapy and wondering all the while if she's getting the correct dosage, the best dosage, the right drug cocktail, etc., etc.

The more you can distract her with all these worries, the more you can keep her from turning to the MH—who, of course, would help her to be at peace with whatever decisions she might make. Worse, She would help your victim to take comfort in her humanness, in the very fact that attaining a guaranteed cure for her cancer is beyond her reach, and to let go of what she can't control. The MH does have the distinct advantage of knowing what it is like to suffer.

Ψ Anesthesia

Subj: Make sure she keeps it to herself
From: Anasty1
To: gnawingirl

Of course she's angry. It's a known byproduct of her condition, so don't start patting yourself on the back for it. She's furious, in fact. That her life (of which every moment has been the MH's gift, but never mind that) may be coming to an end. That she may not get to live to the ripe old age she had planned—it's so unfair, isn't it, the poor thing. And her family and friends are thinking the same thing, but no one is talking to her about it. It's a beautiful thing, the denial of death. She's completely alone with her feelings—and if you've learned anything at all from me, you'll keep her that way.

More than anything, keep her from talking with the MH about her anger, for She would be right there with her in it. She might even show her how to use it to gain the strength and courage she needs now. But if you can get her to waste her energy pretending to all the world that her anger isn't even there, she'll never notice the MH providing for her yet again.

Ψ Anesthesia

Subj: No automatic evils
From: Anasty1
To: gnawingirl

Hospitals, doctor's offices, treatments, and procedures offer many opportunities for pain and fear, but other less desirable outcomes are also possible. The courageous examples of other cancer patients, for instance—all those vulnerable humans caring for each other—may move your victim toward the MH. The usual strategy should be in effect: isolate her. Public waiting rooms, and those chemotherapy treatment bays with several patients together, should always be avoided in favor of more private areas. Be on the lookout for signs of the MH, for She's often found hanging around places like the cancer ward.

Ψ Anesthesia

Subj: The old reliable: human Pride
From: Anasty1
To: gnawingirl

Let her push away those who love her. Like many women, she's used to helping others but unaccustomed to being the helpee. Encourage her to think that even though she's the one who's sick this time, she really doesn't want to bother or upset the people who care about her. Let her be too proud to tell her family and friends what they could do to help. Encourage her to dwell on feelings of humiliation whenever she must ask for assistance. Keep her from realizing that it may now be as much an act of love to ask for a cup of tea as it once was to make a cup of tea for another.

Ψ Anesthesia

Subj: What a nuisance
From: Anasty1
To: gnawingirl

It *is* annoying to begin a promising line of thought with a human, only to be interrupted when she notices the smell of honeysuckle in the air. Annoying but not surprising. Humans who have endured some sort of suffering are generally more able to enjoy the small pleasures of life. Why these two phenomena occur together is quite a puzzle, and I intend to get to the bottom of it. Has your victim begun thanking the MH for little things? Does the sound of a bird chirping, for instance, or a train whistle, please her deeply, more so than ever before? Send me any data you have on this topic for my latest research paper: "Here We Go Again: Use of Suffering As It Applies to the Appreciation of Life."

 Ψ Anesthesia

Subj: It can do plenty
From: Anasty1
To: gnawingirl

Her precious cancer support group is getting to be quite the nuisance, isn't it? Tell you what, next time she goes, let her read that pathetic little poem about what cancer cannot do. There are others in the group, better trained in our attitude toward life, who might be encouraged to react with fury at its sentiments. Perhaps they can even undo your victim's little bit of trusting faith. At the very least they can run her off.

 Ψ Anesthesia

Subj: Letting go is hard to do . . .
From: Anasty1
To: gnawingirl

. . . since she doesn't want to, especially when it comes to her kids. Keep her from remembering the many times she saw the MH providing for her family. Develop such anxiety about her (failing) treatment plan that she forgets she might leave them in the care of the MH. She'll be in such hysteria that you will rob her of the only gift she has left to give her children: the example of how to die well.

    Ψ Anesthesia

Subj: Death
From: Anasty1
To: gnawingirl

I'd forgotten that you've never had the pleasure of watching the death of one of the humans under our control. As one of our own dies, she sees the pure light of the MH beckoning her forward . . . and is terrified of it! And so she turns and runs, a natural reaction to abject terror. As she plunges further and further into the outer darkness she becomes more and more totally ours to enjoy.

    Ψ Anesthesia

Subj: Unpredictable
From: Anasty1
To: gnawingirl

You think you have a victim's fate signed and sealed, only to find her welcoming the light of the MH as she dies. Or you think you've lost one—and then find her shrinking from the rays of truth and mercy, heading straight to us. There is a mysterious quality to the MH, a schizophrenic mixture of justice and kindness—we just never know for sure how a human will react. Yours included.

Ψ Anesthesia

Subj: You're kidding
From: Anasty1
To: gnawingirl

You have really shot yourself in the foot this time. There you are, with a victim who is apparently going to die from her current illness; and instead of attending to her, you're down in the lower levels complaining about me. I will attend to you, Termite, you can count on it. I know all about your claim to have been poorly advised in the case of this victim. I have also heard that you're passing around my latest research proposal as if the idea had originated with you. Ha! You couldn't originate your way out of a paper bag.

Bringing your victim to us is the only answer to your predicament. Forget trying to undercut me—it won't get you off the hook, and it *will* distract you from what should be front and center. Focus all your efforts on your victim and soon you may be enjoying her rather than complaining about *any* aspect of a situation you and you alone have allowed to develop.

Ψ Anesthesia

Subj: You're the one who still doesn't get it
From: Anasty1
To: gnawingirl

You never were the brightest bulb in the chandelier, Termite—I see that all too clearly, if belatedly. But now I'm beginning to wonder if your cord is even plugged in. She's "still ours" because she never got it right? You unmitigated fool. Do you think the MH cares whether she ever got it right? Do you think it matters to Her that you can still, to this day, tempt her to forget Her and follow us? She forgives her, Termite, and She will keep on forgiving her. All that matters to Her is that somehow she keeps returning to Her, keeps desiring Her above us. Her success in the matter is of absolutely no interest to Her. How annoying to have to review such elementary material so late in the game, when there's so much to be done.

ᴪ Anesthesia

Subj: Story time
From: Anasty1
To: gnawingirl

Hello, Termite. Haven't heard from you lately, but I've heard from Licehead's advisor that your victim is spending some time talking with her husband, reflecting on her life's story. Obviously, that's a mistake. A tempter with half a brain wouldn't let anyone near her victim the time and inclination to listen to her, especially anyone who also knows the story of the MH's Son. They might make some unfortunate connections.

Of course, I'm not expecting you to follow my counsel. Too much of my good advice has been ignored throughout the life of this paltry human. And if she goes to the MH upon her demise, I'll have my own story ready: a well-documented description of all your failings. And the oven ready, the table set, to feast on *you* instead. Looking forward to seeing you, in any event.

ᴪ Anesthesia

Ψ Part Six

Appendix A

(Editor's Note: After the death of her intended victim, Termite apparently disappeared. She was subsequently charged with treason, and Anesthesia was charged with aiding and abetting in her escape.

In preparation for Anesthesia's trial, an interview was conducted with Licehead, the tempter assigned to the husband of Termite's intended victim. In his statement, Licehead gave the following eyewitness account of the death of the intended victim, and speculated on Termite's whereabouts.)

Licehead's Statement

I was with my victim in his bedroom as he sat there watching his wife die, and it's a wonder I didn't die myself—from nausea. She'd fade back into consciousness, ask for her husband, weakly grasp his hand, and bring up some meaningless memory that made them both smile. Or she'd wake up, just long enough to croak out some banality along the lines of "thank you" or "life has been good, hasn't it?" before drifting off again. Other friends and family were in and out of her room too. Often there were smiles mixed with tears during the goodbyes, and occasionally a soft word of apology or forgiveness. It was obnoxious beyond any possible description.

I kept wondering where Termite was and why she didn't do something to stop all this wretched peacefulness. It was not until the day her victim died that I realized what she was up to. First, the room became very still, and another Presence began filling it. Then came the victim's last words, another "thank you," whispered to Her. And then the light in the room grew intensely bright—so bright that I was forced to turn away (and begin my dignified departure, of course).

As I was leaving I heard another sound—it was odd, like a baby's first words, and faint, but I could make the words out: "Please, me too." That's all I heard, but it was enough. Termite went with her, I know she did. She's not hiding out somewhere down here, she has gone with her victim to the MH.

And I know where she got the idea, too. It was from those letters of that crazy Anesthesia—her aunt, can you believe she would say that—everybody knows she is loony tunes from the word go. Termite once showed me some of her h-mails, no doubt they are still on her computer if you need the evidence. One of them even mentions the idea of redemption for us. I have never come across this disgusting notion—and if sharing *that* with an impressionable young tempter isn't crazy, I don't know what is. I'll tell you one thing, the two of them—Termite and Anesthesia—did such a lousy job that *their* victim actually did some damage in the life of mine. I deserve a piece of Anesthesia just to make up for the problems they've caused me.

Licehead